Angst in the Arms of Morpheus

By N. A. Rushton

ISBN: 9781917425377 (Hardback)

9781917293860 (Paperback)

Chapter I

Night had already cloaked the skies with darkness when Jonathan's parents pulled up outside his new apartment building. They had been driving for nearly six hours and were all exhausted.

Jonathan looked from the car window, thoughtfully up at the tall apartment block that was to be his abode for the next couple of years, wondering what his future held. A hectic few days to begin with, he felt sure. Luckily for him, the apartment he was renting was fully furbished, so all he needed to do was unpack his clothes. He would never have had the energy to move any kind of furniture in, no matter how large or small. Neither would his parents, by the look of them.

He'd decided to only pack clothes, as he had thought it would be much easier to buy anything else he might need when he was here. He hadn't taken into account the possibility they might not arrive till late in the evening after many of the shops would have closed. It was Sunday, after all, and he really should have had the foresight for that.

He kept his gaze on the building before him, black against the night, with just a handful of yellow squares, like beacons, indicating any sign of life. This was to be his sanctuary for the next few years whilst he was attending the local University.

The rent on the apartment was being paid for by his parents, who he felt sure had only offered to drive him so that they had an excuse to look at the place in more detail to see if they approved.

The following morning, Jonathan's parents had set off early. Six a.m. early, as they had a six-hour long return journey. So, as he was now up, he took the opportunity to unpack and settle in better. He thought he might as well take the opportunity to go register for his course as well, as, once that was done and out of the way he'd be able to have some time to get some groceries in.

Spending a good while looking around the local area, searching for take-aways, coffee shops and other such conveniences, he chose one of the coffee shops he liked the look of best, and went in to have breakfast.

The coffee was wonderful. Rich, but with a smoothness to it and a berry fruit jam aftertaste that washed down the bacon, lettuce and tomato sandwich he'd ordered with it perfectly.

It had a nice ambience to it too, light Bossanova jazz drifting faintly through the air in the background synchronised with the wispy steam that floated from the hot coffee cup. The shop was quiet but with a comfortable buzz of activity to it. One that was evident, but not disruptive. He felt this might be just the place to make a regular haunt. It was already stimulating his mind into activity, running away with itself on the subject matter of his studies.

Breakfast finished, he made his way towards the university so he could get the job of signing up for his course out of the way, then he would move on to more pressing concerns.

As he made his way there, he couldn't help but notice, eerily so, how few people of his own age group he could see. He had expected an enthusiastic throng of likeminded students out and about, generating a hive of activity. He felt certain that he'd have an opportunity to make the acquaintance of some of them, maybe even make some friends. Not that he was overly confident in that regard. He had never been any good at starting conversations with complete strangers, still, he felt this was the least daunting setting in which to do so, and therefore one of the best opportunities afforded to him.

When he arrived to enrol, he was even more shocked to find he was the only one there, aside from the people doing the enrolment. The auditorium was ghostly silent, and he felt a pang of doubt building up in his stomach, like a small ball was stuck in his gut, growing larger by the minute. It was leaning itself against his nerves, the pressure of it building slowly till the nerves and the doubts were of equal magnitude. Was he at the right place? Was he too early? Had he made some kind of mistake?

The lady at the desk looked directly at him, focused, like an owl that had seen a distance field mouse. She really had no option; other than her colleague he was the only other person in the room.

Then he heard the door open behind him. A flood of relief washed over him as he saw a girl entering, like a minor tornado, seemingly full of confidence and enthusiasm, who asked.

"Is this where we enrol for the Psychology course?"

"Yes. I think so." Jonathan replied. The girl did a brief double take, as though she had only just noticed him. Clearly, she hadn't directed her question at him, in spite of him answering,

"Are you sitting psychology too?" she asked.

"Err, yes." He returned, a little nervously.

"You sure? you don't sound too certain."

Jonathan didn't know how to respond and flushed crimson with embarrassment.

"I'm only winding you up," she replied laughing "have you enrolled already?"

Jonathan smiled uncertainly and tried to regain his composure.

"No, not yet. I was just about to." and with that he turned and approached the lady at the desk.

"Looks like being a small class, eh?" the girl said from behind him a moment later, while the lady busied herself with her duties.

"Oh, no. I think the rest will enrol later. We're just early I think."

The girl was laughing to herself.

"Really!?" she replied, with a heavy tone of sarcasm.

"Yes...oh" he replied, realising she wasn't being serious, and that he had just been too slow to cotton on.

"I'm Jennifer." she said, holding her hand out, smiling.

He gently, and with a great deal of uncertainty, in case this was another joke of some kind, shook her hand.

"Jonathan."

"No. Jennifer!" she replied, dead pan. But she couldn't contain herself for too long, and another big smile began to slowly creep across her face. It was such a genuine smile that Jonathan was instantly disarmed. He couldn't help noticing her whole face lit up with it.

Jonathan just looked at her confused. He had no idea how to take this girl. She seemed nice enough, but he also felt as though she were constantly mocking him. He'd have to be careful around her, he thought, he had experienced too many bullies like this in his past.

After a moment he noticed she was still looking directly at him. Not in the general way people look at one another when they are talking to them. It was an intense fixed look. She was scrutinising him, and he knew exactly why.

"Can I ask you something personal?" she asked, still staring at him.

Here it comes, he thought.

"Do you have to?" he replied, a little forlornly. It was like he was going through Deja-vu.

"You get asked a lot, eh?" this seemed a genuinely curious question.

"What do you think?" he replied.

"It does look a bit odd though. You must admit?"

"I can't help how I look."

"You could cut it off? It wouldn't look any worse. I mean, you kind of do look like a tennis ball that's been used too much."

If Jonathan wasn't appreciating her mocking before, he certainly wasn't now. It was history repeating, he had received the exact same comments everywhere. Sometimes more politely put, often less so.

Feeling a little dejected at the poor start to his university life, he decided that it would be best if he no longer engage her in conversation and simply turned and walked away.

"I'm off. I've some shopping to do." he said, trying, and failing, to act as though it wasn't just an excuse to end what was, for him, yet another uncomfortable conversation.

"Oh, don't be like that. I didn't mean anything by it. I was only asking. I'm sorry."

"It's okay. I really do have some shopping I need to do. I'm sure I'll see you around campus." he replied, thinking 'but I'll be doing my best to avoid you' and with that he left.

Jennifer watched him leave. She really hadn't mean to upset him, but when you look as unusual as he did, it was only natural to be inquisitive. To not be you would really have to have something wrong with you. Still, she didn't mean to offend him, and she had already begun to feel guilty for not broaching the subject a little more sensitively - if there even was a way to do that - so she followed on after him in the hope of trying to make peace.

Jennifer spent the first half of the journey to the supermarket half apologising, half trying to explain her natural curiosity. Eventually Jonathan acquiesced and forgave her, at which point the conversation lost its edge and they began talking about normal subjects once again.

She explained that she too had arrived late the previous night; although she was in the halls of residence and that she was still yet to meet her room mates. They had a laugh over what they might be like.

"So, what do you need?" Jennifer asked as they entered the food court.

"Just the basics for now. Tea, coffee, milk, sugar, bread, some tins of stuff, beans, soup, that sort of thing. Maybe some pasta, a sauce to go with it and some meat. Maybe sausages. I can always come back later for other stuff."

"We should have brought my car," Jennifer replied "we could have done a big shop for both of us."

"Never mind. I wanted to get my bearings anyway. It'll be useful to know where things are and walking it helps get the layout of the land."

Jennifer looked at Jonathan with no small sense of intrigue. To be so organised, and to have such foresight impressed her. She was much more of a 'last minute, oh, I nearly forgot' type of person. Much to her own annoyance on many an occasion.

"Well, once you've done your shopping, I'll grab my car and we can come back, and you can help me do mine. Deal?" she replied, hopefully.

"Yeah, sure."

"So, you found any other useful places?" she continued, wanting to keep the conversation going.

"A coffee shop, a cafe. I just need to find a bookshop or two and somewhere to get stationary and I'm pretty much set for all the essentials."

"No pubs?"

"Nah, not yet I don't think they're really essentials, and I'm sure they'll find themselves easy enough."

"You're pretty clued up, aren't you?" she said, and looked him over in a reevaluating kind of fashion "I like you." she continued with a nod of her head as though agreeing with her own assessment.

Jonathan was lost for words. It wasn't often he got compliments, even rarer that someone admitted to actually liking him, and he was unsure how to respond.

"Thanks?" he said, tentatively.

They finished shopping and carried everything back to Jonathan's apartment. The bags strained to contain their contents and threatened to break at any moment. Being so much bulkier than he had expected, Jennifer took the lightest bag, and Jonathan carried the two heavier ones, which seemed fair as it was his shopping. By the time they had got back he could hardly feel his fingers from where the handles had been digging in.

Jonathan, quickly unloading everything, in a rather disordered fashion, into the fridge and cupboards, they then headed straight back out so that Jennifer might retrieve her car so she could sort out some provisions for herself.

Jennifer bought much the same things as Jonathan had, it seemed the easier option for her as it meant she didn't have to think too much about what to get. The main difference being that she also bought some fruit as well.

The room at the halls of residence, where Jennifer was staying, was larger than Jonathan had expected it to be, although it was empty when they arrived. As soon as they actually went inside it, it didn't seem quite as big as he had at first thought.

Trying to imagine a third person in here, as Jennifer had mentioned she was sharing with two others, he soon thought it might be somewhat cramped after all.

"Shall we go out for lunch?" asked Jennifer.

"Are you sure?" Jonathan asked. "We've only just spent all this money on food."

"I know, but I don't want to eat on my own. I thought we might get something to eat and go look for a bookshop or two?"

Jonathan sensed that, as confident as this girl tried to appear, she was faking it, and she had an aversion to being on her own. He sensed a vulnerability in her that he hadn't seen previously. Maybe her mocking him was an attempt on her part to cover up her own feelings of vulnerability? He cast the idea to one side as it seemed too odd a tactic.

All that considered, he still didn't want to be spending money eating out all the time, especially as they had both just bought a few days' worth of food. He had only been at university for a day and already he was at risk of spending too frivolously, which was not a habit he wanted to get into. It was going to be costly enough as it was without adding to it unnecessarily.

"Let's compromise," he replied "we can go eat at my place and from there we can go book shopping?"

"Yeah, alright." agreed Jennifer. A little quickly, Jonathan thought.

They took Jennifers car, which he thought was a bit lazy on their part as it was only a relatively short distance for them, but Jennifer pointed out that it would make bookshop hunting that much easier and give them a greater catchment area in which they could explore. Jonathan saw the sense in that.

Chapter II

Jennifer hadn't entered Jonathan's apartment when they had been here earlier. She had stayed at the doorstep for the few minutes that it had taken him to put his shopping away, but now she was inside she was quite taken aback by how large it was.

The entrance led directly into the living room. There was a coffee table in the centre with a couch to its right and an armchair at the far end. The armchair had a quilted throwover on it, and it looked incredibly comfortable.

Immediately behind it was a tall reading lamp. One of those where you could adjust its snakelike neck into, more or less, any conceivable position due to its coiled upper shaft. The wire from the base of the lamp disappearing under a large rug behind the chair, and emerged the other side, running along the skirting board leading behind a five or six foot long sideboard that contained a vase of plastic flowers, a television and a stack of books.

In the opposite corner was a desk which contained a computer and another stack of books. To the side of that was the kitchen area. Her eyes followed the room around to a door in the corner immediately to the right of her.

Although the door was closed, she presumed that led off to the bedroom, or bedrooms.

"This is a nice apartment you have. How do you afford this?"

"I don't," Jonathan replied from the kitchen. "My parents pay the rent."

"That's good of them."

"Not really, if I don't pass my exams, I have to pay them back every penny."

"Really?" Jennifer asked, a little incredulous.

"Their idea of motivation."

"Wow! Sucks to be you." she replied, then decided it might be better to change the subject.

"So, What's cooking?"

"Pasta and sauce with some sausages. I might slice them up, it'll make it look more than it is."

"Sounds delish!" she replied, then, realising that that sounded sarcastic, added "I have that all the time at home."

Catching the look Jonathan was giving her, she sensed that that hadn't sound any better.

"That didn't come out right." Jennifer said apologetically.

"Really? was it actually supposed to sound insulting?"

Jonathan had only known Jennifer a few hours and already he got the impression that this foot-in-mouth behaviour was just her way, and that she really didn't mean to be insulting or offensive, it was just the way things came out. She was one of those people who, whatever they said, they always sounded like they were mocking you. Whether any of it was intentional or not, he would probably never be able to discern. So, he decided he would accept her for who she was and be done with it.

Strangely, he found that this also seemed to embolden him to be uncharacteristically cheekier than was his nature.

"I'll stop talking." she replied a little timidly.

Jonathan couldn't contain the cough of laughter that erupted from him spontaneously.

Jennifer also laughed; it was contagious. The tension that had begun to build immediately alleviated.

They ate in silence, neither quite able to think of anything that wasn't inane that they might use to resurrect some form of conversation.

"That was really nice." Jennifer said when they had finished and were clearing the dishes away. Jonathan couldn't tell if she was being sincere or just being polite. It hinted at 'that was just about edible, I hope you haven't poisoned me', but given how forthright she had been so far, he thought she would probably say that without remorse if it was truly the case.

"Thanks. I'll just get these washed up then we can get on out. You have a look online while I get them done."

Jennifer wasn't going to pass up an opportunity to avoid doing any washing up, so, while Jonathan did that, she set about searching the internet for bookshops.

She found three, all within a one-mile radius; the closest of which was only a hundred or so yards from the University itself. What was even better, was that it was also not much further than that from her dorm.

"We'll do this one first," she said to Jonathan, as he emerged from the kitchen and approached the desk, peering over her shoulder as she pointed at the screen. "Then we can go over to that one, and then finish off back over here to this one. That looks to be closer to the city centre, so we can check out some of the bars once we've done."

"What are their closing times?" he asked.

"Why? We've plenty of time, it's only one o'clock."

"Yes, but if one of them closes at two o'clock for some reason, or even three, we should do that one first."

"What kind of shop closes at two?"

"One that opens very early or opens at weekends." he replied, as though that were blatantly obvious.

She checked the opening and closing hours of each of the bookshops. Two opened at eight, the other at eight thirty, and they closed at four thirty, five thirty and six p.m. Respectively.

"We should do that one first" said Jonathan, pointing to the one that closed earliest.

"You think we're going to spend over three hours in one bookshop?"

"Depends if it has anything we need," he replied "and it depends on just how big a bookshop it is. I've been in ones that are three floors high and have hundreds of thousands of books available; and, if they have a cafe in them, that could easily add an extra thirty to forty minutes to our trip."

"Okay. We'll do them in the order they close, " she replied, not being overly bothered about the order, but hoping they didn't end up spending three or four hours in them. "I just need to nip to the loo before we set off."

As soon as they entered the first bookshop, Jennifer began to wonder if Jonathan hadn't already been here. It was almost exactly as he had described.

From the outside, it didn't look too big. A typical shop front, maybe ten meters in width, with a window display of various recently published books, plus a few less recent but popular ones. But, on entering, she saw that it was huge!

The floor they were on went all the way back to the furthest end of the building, which must have been sixty or seventy meters long. The flooring, a citrus yellowy orange with a pomegranate red carpet marking the walkway.

Each wall was lined with shelf after shelf of books, with additional shelves projecting out perpendicularly in a huge broken toothed comb-like fashion that created separate open box like spaces. The first of which she could see contained a medium sized table in its centre which was also laden with books, almost as though in solidarity with the overworked shelves.

Immediately to their left were the service desks, where three people were attending to customers who were queuing at the tills, and about twenty meters further along the floor from them was a sign hanging from the ceiling indicating staircases leading both up and downwards to different floors.

"Oh, my word!" exclaimed Jennifer quietly "where do we even start?"

Jonathan, who although a little taken aback by the sheer magnitude of the place, smiled approvingly, and took a moment before replying.

"I'd say we probably try find the psychology section first." He said, sensibly.

"We should split up. It'll be quicker." replied Jennifer, suddenly realising that it could very easily take them three hours if they stayed together to look. "Here, give me your mobile number so we can call each other when we find it."

After exchanging phone numbers, they agreed that Jonathan would take the lower floor while Jennifer remained on this floor. They would meet up at the stairwell in an hour if neither of them had found what they were looking for any sooner.

As Jonathan went off in the direction of the stairs, Jennifer began casting her eyes over the shelves to the right of her in much greater earnest than before. This section contained Authors A-Z and appeared to be the Z end of the alphabet. Twisting her head to the side she read some of the titles. One in particular caught her eye 'The Shadow of the Wind' by Carlos Ruis Zafon. She liked the poetic resonance of the title, and the authors name had a similar musical cadence to it. At least it did the way she was saying it.

She eased open the hard cover so she could read the blurb in the inside of the dust jacket. After a casual read through, she tucked it under her arm and carried on making her way down the shelves, trying hard not to read many of the titles, as she knew she would end up spending her whole months allowance if she didn't exercise some restraint.

She worked her way past the T's, then S, and managed to get all the way down to K before another title caught her eye. 'The Sound of the Mountain'. This had the same poetic ring to it that 'Shadow of the Wind' had. She scanned through a few pages and, deciding that she liked the look of this one as well, placed it under her arm with the other.

This was no good. She was only supposed to be looking for the psychology section, but the allure of the bookshop had her already buying two books that she hadn't initially had any inclination of buying, and at this rate she'd be overloaded before she even found psychology. She needed to be more focused and get away from the Fiction section.

She ignored the books themselves and just looked for general topics. Behind her were biographies and political books. Neither of which did she have any interest in, which helped; so she just headed straight to the very back of the store so see what was there.

More fiction, although this area was dedicated to Horror and Science Fiction.

Checking the time, she was alarmed to see that she had spent a full fifty minutes looking around.

She headed towards the stairs to meet up with Jonathan.

Jennifer had only taken two steps when her phone pinged. It was a text message from Jonathan.

'Found it, finally. Meet at top of stairs.'

She made her way directly to him.

"What kept you?" he asked, when she arrived.

"What do you mean? I only just got your text."

"Really? I sent that fifteen minutes ago."

"Must be the reception in here," she replied, a little dismayed "Go on then, lead the way."

Jonathan led her down the stairs and along the floor to an area labelled 'Psychology'. Almost as a mirror of the floor above, there were shelves coming out at right angles from the wall and the Psychology books were situated inside one of the alcoves that this created, so you had to go into it and look back in order to see those shelves.

There was a blond-haired girl huddled into the corner, flipping through a book.

"Here." Jonathan said to Jennifer.

"Wow. They have quite a selection, but not the easiest to find."

"Yeah. Here this is one of the one's we need for the course." replied Jonathan, picking a book off the shelf.

"Oh, there's only one copy." Jennifer said,

"No, there's two." replied Jonathan, matter of factly. Then he noticed the blond-haired girl was holding the other one.

"Excuse me. Are you planning on buying that book?" he asked politely.

"Hmm??" the girl replied, clearly not paying attention. "What was that, sorry?"

"Are you planning on buying that book?"

"Oh, yes. I need it for my university course." she replied, smiling.

"Us too!" interjected Jennifer. "Are you studying Psychology as well?"

"Yes," replied the girl, a little more enthusiastically this time.

"My name is Jennifer, this is Jonathan. Have you registered yet?"

"Yes. I've just come from there."

"Oh, we'll be in the same class." Jennifer with a certain level of glee. Jonathan noticed Jennifer was somewhat more enthusiastic about making a new female friend than she had been with him.

"Where are you staying?" Jennifer continued.

"Halls of residence, to begin with, but I'm looking for a flat of my own already. I'm just finding my bearings at the moment, getting settled in. But as soon as I have, I'll be looking for a part time job and then flat hunting. I'd prefer to get settled somewhere a bit more permanent if I can. It's stressful enough just moving in now."

"I know what you mean," Jennifer replied "Jonathan here has his own apartment already. What's your name?"

"Elizabeth."

"Pleased to meet you Elizabeth," then, turning to Jonathan "well, we've found what we're looking for here, shall we bother with the others? or call it a day and find somewhere to relax.

Elizabeth, who, since Jennifer had mentioned Jonathan had his own apartment, had not taken her eyes off him and was still looking at Jonathan, making him feel a little nervous again. He had an inkling that he knew what was going through her mind. It would be the same as he had gone through with Jennifer just an hour or so earlier. He decided it might be best to excuse themselves from her and go their separate ways. He was in no mood to go through that again so soon.

Elizabeth however, on hearing that Jonathan had his own apartment, decided Jonathan would be the perfect person to help her flat hunting. If he had his own place already, he would know the places to go, the places to look and the people whom she might need to speak to. So, she made it a priority to make friends with him as soon as she possibly could.

"I think it best if we stick to our original plan. We have plenty of time and it'll be good to see what they have on offer as well," he turned to Elizabeth, who was still looking at him with a smile on her face that made him think of a spider looking at a fly that was flying around its web. "Well, lovely meeting you." he said bluntly, and took a step to signal to Jennifer that they should be on their way.

"There's other bookshops around here?" Elizabeth asked, "I thought this was the only one?"

"Oh, no!" Jennifer interjected before Jonathan could speak. "there's two others".

"I wouldn't mind checking them out too. Do you mind if I tag along?"

"Not at all." replied Jennifer, smiling.

They spent the next few hours traveling from one bookshop to the other, taking note of where each of the pubs were, along with various other social establishments essential for student life.

Elizabeth vainly kept attempting to introduce flat hunting into the conversation, but Jennifer, seemingly oblivious to her voice, kept changing the subject onto something utterly germane, ranging from where each of them were from originally, who their favourite actors were, their favourite films and why, then, somehow the conversation moved onto which pub they would have their first night out at. It then weaved its way onto who their first boyfriend or girlfriend was and how that came about.

Eventually the topic of conversation once again wound its way back to student life. Elizabeth desperately jumped at the opportunity to try re-introduce the topic of buying a flat.

"Imagine being able to afford University without student loans and handouts from our parents." she said, as casually as she was able to, pushing open the door to the final bookshop.

It was an old looking second-hand bookshop - whether it was genuinely old or just made to look old they couldn't really tell. It had that old bookshop smell, which gave it a note of authenticity. Their nostrils caught the scent the moment they stepped inside, the door closing behind them,

"Oh, smell that," said Elizabeth, with a level of glee to her voice. "All that's missing is the aroma of fresh brewed coffee, and it'd be perfect."

"Smells musty to me." Jennifer replied, unimpressed.

"I love it!" Elizabeth replied, gazing around.

The entrance way led into a large open space, around ten yards by ten yards, with very old, mahogany looking, ornate bookshelves lining the walls. Each one, crammed with books. In the centre were positioned two tables, similarly old looking and matching the shelves in design. These tables were about a yard or so apart and laden with crumpled, raggedy looking cardboard boxes that were also crammed full of paperback books. There didn't appear to be any kind of order to them, they were just dumped lazily into place, wherever they could fit, spines facing upwards so that prospective buyers might be able to read the titles - those of which that were in a good enough state for the title to be read, that is. Many were so well used they were just creme coloured mesh for a spine.

This was clearly the 'bargain bucket' selection.

The books on the shelves were in much better condition, many of them looking as though they were brand new, albeit a little on the dusty side. They gave an odd appearance. All lined, perfectly level and even, as though the utmost care had been taken that they were placed as neatly, and orderly as possible, but all covered in a fog of dust, as though they had been abandoned utterly. Quite the dichotomy.

Further ahead was another entrance that led up a couple of bare wooden steps into a back room of sorts, and this was where the antiquarian books appeared to be housed. Elizabeth thought that even the newest book in this area must have been well over a hundred years old, and she made her way deeper into the room. Jennifer and Jonathan followed.

There was only one other customer in the shop at the time, and he looked to be engrossed in a very thick, heavy looking volume of some description. His long silky black beard making him look younger than his feint yellowy tanned skin and threadbare old clothing would otherwise indicate.

They paid him no further regard, and carried on looking around,

Elizabeth was still eager to discuss the finding a flat, so tried to navigate the conversations back to where it had just been.

"Where were we?" she asked.

"What?" replied Jennifer.

"Book smells." Jonathan said.

"No, before that." Elizabeth replied.

"Oh. You were saying how good it would be to be able to afford University without loans or handouts." replied Jonathan.

"Oh, that would be a dream come true!" Elizabeth replied and was about to go on to mention her flat hunting interests to get Jonathan's opinions, when the customer, as though triggered by the topic of their conversation, lowered his book slightly and transferred his attention to them.

"What makes you say such a thing?" he asked. His accent was difficult to place, but his voice was calm and smooth, philosophical even, but with the faintest hint of annoyance behind it.

"Beg your pardon?" Jennifer said, caught unawares by the stranger.

"You say it would be a dream come true. What makes you say such a thing?"

"Well, because it would be," replied Jennifer, confused. "To not be in debt for years to come, what could be bad about that?"

"You ever had a nightmare? They are dreams also. What if they came true?"

"Well...that..." Jennifer stuttered.

"Mind your own business." Jonathan said abruptly, cutting Jennifer off. He took offence at some random stranger interjecting himself into their conversation, especially when he was saying things that seemed to have an air of threat to them, as he just had. It filled him with a strange confidence to challenge this stranger in such a fashion, and was uncharacteristically rude for Jonathan.

Clearly the stranger was not accustomed to being spoken to in such an abrupt and forthright fashion, and, whilst remaining stoically expressionless, he fixed Jonathan with such a gaze that, were it possible to do so with a single vicious glance, he would obliterate Jonathan from the face of the planet.

Jonathan tried to match the intensity of the man's gaze as best he could. He wasn't used to such confrontationalism, but he forced himself to add a very determined challenge of his own to the exchange. He had no idea where he found such aggression from, but the stranger backed down eventually and returned his attention back to his book, closing it gently, and quietly uttered.

"As you wish." as he turned and made his way towards the register to pay for his book. On doing so, he made towards the shop door, turned and said,

"Three hundred and thirty-three days from now, your dreams will come to fruition." And with that, he left the shop.

As soon as they saw the door close behind him, they collectively let out a long-held breath. Jonathan calmed down a little, and turned his attention back towards the girls.

"You okay?" he asked "I hate it when people do that. What makes him think he can just butt into other people's conversations? How rude!"

"You didn't need to be quite so rude yourself though. What if he'd gotten angry and attacked us?" Jennifer said a touch cautiously. She had only known Jonathan only a few hours and this was the first time she had seen his temper piqued. She found it a little thrilling but wanted to tread carefully until he had calmed down more.

Jonathan said nothing. He just turned and wandered around the shop looking randomly at the shelves, as though nothing had happened. He still needed to calm down and let the adrenalin that was pulsing through his bloodstream abate. Eventually, the emotions of the confrontation dissipated, and they put it behind them, continuing with their afternoon.

From the bookshop, they found a coffee shop and picked up their random and rather eclectic conversations over coffee and a snack before making their way on to a nearby pub.

It was past eleven o'clock before they finally called it a night, went their separate ways and got some much-needed sleep.

It had been a long, busy day and they had several more ahead of them before they got fully settled into student life.

One thing they did know for sure; that day they had each made friends of each other for life.

Chapter III

Jonathan was, almost, your typical student at the University of _______. However, as had previously been alluded to, he had one distinguishing characteristic, and that was the onset of male pattern baldness. It was an affliction that had plagued every male member of his family for generations past, and he was no exception.

It had been a source of a great deal of torment for him. He had first noticed this affliction when he was just sixteen years old, and had been distraught at the first realisation that the hair on the top of his head was not as thick as once it had been. At first, he thought it might just have been a trick of the light, that the hair at the sides of his head looked fuller and thicker by comparison due to some optical illusion; but after several minutes of contorting himself one way and then another so as to obtain a better position in which to look, trying multiple different angles and using a mirror, he had to face the stark reality that his pate was thinning.

At some point a year or so prior, when he'd had what might be considered a normal head of hair, he had made the decision to grow it long, in a juvenile attempt to emulate his favourite musician. Spending months allowing the length to grow out, he found he was cursed for it to merely grow bushier and bushier, instead of longer. The true length only being revealed when his hair got wet, such as at the swimming baths, at which point it would be unfurled, like Rapunzel, by the weight of the water and be drawn down to the middle of his shoulder blades; only then to be contracted back to the thick matt of hair when the chlorinated water disbursed, and his hair began to dry again.

He cursed the misfortunes of having curly hair, especially as the idol whom he was attempting to emulate did not - sadly, he also lacked the foresight to realise that this infatuation of said individual would be so short-lived, and replaced a few months later by a different celebrity, which would subsequently also be a short-lived infatuation. Such lack of clairvoyance of the fleeting idolisations of individuals being the curse of many a youth.

However, at that point in time, his curly hair was the source of much frustration for him. When he finally succumbed to the pressure from his parents to finally get a haircut, his affliction was finally revealed to him, much to his chagrin. It seemed he was to be constantly suffering with regret in one form or another.

He wasn't the only one to notice his affliction either.

As if it were not bad enough for a then sixteen-year-old to return to school with a new haircut, especially one so drastic as his, but for it also to be evident that the poor child was also beginning to thin on top, left him ripe for the ridiculing comments that any wannabe comedian in the school wished to inflict upon him whenever they saw fit. And they saw fit rather often, and mercilessly so.

For three years he endured these torments from his classmates, and, though they did diminish in magnitude somewhat, over time, they never really disappeared. This left him feeling alienated, alone, and hating pretty much everything about the way he looked.

By nineteen years of age, and still in his first term at university, he had decided, after many comments from fellow students, including his only two friends, to take some semblance of control of the situation and had gone to task on the patchy hair and thinning pate that so disturbed him.

He knew full well it was pure vanity that exercised its dominance over his ego, but at nineteen he wanted to be able to fit in more with his fellow students, feel a more accepted component of the community, and so felt he had few alternative options at hand.

By way of an attempt to compensate for his genetically induced baldness, Jonathan had also decided to grow a beard. This had also proved to be a futile endeavour. The beard resembling something akin to how you might imagine a child to look if they were to shave an animal and then attempt to glue said shavings to their chin and jawline.

That is to say that, to every onlooker outside of himself, he looked...odd.

Nevertheless, he felt it gave him a certain gravitas and a level of maturity that would otherwise be lacking from his persona were he to remain cleanshaven.

After an initial period of confoundedness, and a similarly short period of adjustment, his friends accepted that this was the way he wished to present himself to the world, and they became accustomed to it, and, in fact, oblivious. A case of familiarity breeding acceptance, if you will.

This is, however, a digression from the actual tale, so allow me to navigate back to it.

The events that initiated the series of fortunes, and misfortunes, of young Jonathan occurred on a snowy evening, a year later and late one autumn, as he walked and talked with two of his university friends, Elizabeth and Jennifer, down the high street a short way away from the university itself.

Their conversation had been, as was usually the case when he spent time with them, somewhat eclectic - Ranging from philosophical contemplations, to local University gossip, to more mundane topics such as what they were planning on watching on television that night - when the conversation, bouncing and colliding from topic to topic as it was want, finally settled on the idea that Christmas was only a month or so away.

"Have you thought about what gifts you are buying everyone for Christmas?" asked Elizabeth.

"Oh. No," replied Jennifer "there's loads of time yet. I won't start for another couple of weeks."

"I'm horrendous at buying gifts," said Jonathan "I always think I've bought something incredibly nice, and then they open it and hate it. Do you remember last year when I bought Helen a relaxation bath set? I thought it would be just the thing for her, you know how stressed and highly strung she gets, it seemed like the ideal gift, you know, help her relax a little and de-stress. But did you see how her face fell when she opened it? you'd have thought I'd just killed her dog! ... She thought I didn't notice, but I did. I was mortified."

"Did she?" said Elizabeth " I didn't notice. I remember the gift. I thought it was lovely. I'd have loved to have got something like that. I love those relaxing bath bombs and stuff. Are you sure she didn't like it?"

"Oh, I do. She rewrapped it and gave it to her mother for her Birthday a month or so later." said Jennifer, and the three of them burst out laughing.

"Oh well, at least someone liked it" said Jonathan between laughs.

"Well, I've bought five gifts already," said Elizabeth, after she'd stopped laughing, "I like to have everything ready in good time. I can't do with all that last minute rushing about and panicking a few days before Christmas."

"Thats usually me," said Jonathan "but not this year. I've made a promise to myself to have everything ready and wrapped for the week before. I've had my eyes open for gift ideas for people for a few days already. I've just had so little time to go out and have a proper look. I might go do a bit of window shopping this weekend if either of you want to come along?"

"Count me out," replied Jennifer "far too early for Christmas talk for my liking. But if you're going to start, why not start here." she said, nodding her head towards a row of shops that formed a parade, just in front of them.

Ahead of them on the street was an old looking bric-a-brac shop, with a window full of all sorts of items.

"How long has that been here?" asked Elizabeth, with a look of faint confusion on her face.

"Looks like forever." replied Jennifer, casting her eye over the aged appearance of the outside.

"It can't have been. This place has always been empty, don't you remember, there's the bookshop back there" said Elizabeth, pointing behind them. "Then there's the coffee shop, then the shoe shop. Here's the stationary shop, next to us, then it's the empty shop...which it seems is now this. Then there's that pretend English Tea shop that never seems to be open, then the Chinese market just up there." she continued, counting them off, one by one.

"Yes, now that you mention it, it has always been empty." replied Jonathan, suddenly recollecting a conversation they'd had the year before. "Hadn't it burned down, years ago, or something?"

"That's right!" said Jennifer, who's memory was fast returning, pulling through half remembered fragments of many a past conversation. "Did you guys get told the rumour about how it got burned down?" she asked.

"Rumour? what rumour?" asked Jonathan

"It's nothing really. Just one of those silly stories people try telling to scare you, but it wouldn't scare a fourth grader..."

"Well?! go on then" said Jonathan after a moments silence.

"Yes, go on," said Elizabeth "you have to tell us now, you can't just dangle a carrot like that and leave us hanging. Spill the beans."

Jennifer, noting their interest, began to have mischievous thoughts, and decided she would have some fun at their expense and try to recite the story she had been told at the freshman party last year, only embellish it a little to make it better and actually scare them. She would see if she could get them too scared to go inside.

She stopped smiling and took on the most serious face she could muster.

"Well," she began, as all good works of campfire horror fiction should, with the air of authenticity.

"It's said that fifty or so years ago this was a shop that sold all sorts of religious paraphernalia. From all kinds of religions relics from Buddhist temples in Cambodia, Hindu Temples of India, even old Viking charms and bracelets. That sort of thing, and downstairs in the basement, it is said they kept occult items of the 'dark arts'." on saying this, Jennifer could see the expression on Elizabeth and Jonathan's face become a little less jovial, and a lot more concentrated and serious.

She could tell she was reeling them in, and lowered her voice further, in an attempt to build up the tension.

"It is said that they kept evil books of spells and incantations, along with dolls that they could use to put a hex on someone, along with all the ingredients that you might need. Preserved foetus', ground bones of exotic animals, vials of the blood of virgins, pentagrams. They even kept a goat, for ritual slaughter. The owners themselves, it was said, were demons in human skin and they would routinely kidnap the homeless and use them for the sacrifices to their lord and master. They were found out when they took a student by accident. One night, while walking home from a party, a random student had stopped outside, feeling like they were going to throw up, and had fallen asleep in the doorway. The demons, on their nightly search for their next sacrifice, had found the student and grabbed him, not realising that he wasn't actually homeless, and that people would come looking for him. Which is exactly what his housemates did the next day. After spending the full day searching, one of them mentioned the rumours about the shop owners' nefarious activities and after a short time arguing, they decided amongst themselves that their friend had been kidnapped by the shop owners and, as it was on their friend's way back home, they decided to break in to search the property and have a look for evidence.

They waited for nightfall, so as to have less chance of being seen breaking in, and after picking the lock, made their way into the shop. They crept around looking for any evidence they may find of their friend being there; keeping as quiet as they could so they would be able to hear anyone else who might still be in there and reduce their chances of being discovered themselves. Eventually, they decided to creep downstairs to the basement. Naturally, they knew the rumours about what went on in that cellar, so were understandably scared witless. If there hadn't have been three of them, they would never have gone.

Making their way to the door at the back of the shop that led down to the basement, they could see it was open, ever so slightly. Very slowly, so as not to make a noise, they pushed the door further and further open. Peering their heads around the door frame so that they could see down a staircase, at the bottom of which they saw another doorway through which they could see the faint flickering of a light of some description. Still moving slowly, not wanting to make any sound that might give them away, they crept down the wooden stairs…"

Jennifer could see they were both listening intently, and were well and truly drawn in. Neither of them seemed to breath, nor blink. She lowered her voice further, building the tension all the more.

"When they got to the bottom of the steps," Jennifer continued, now leaning in, talking at a level barely above a whisper so as to give the impression she was sharing something of the utmost secrecy that no-one else must know. "They peered round the doorway, and what they saw caused their blood to freeze. Their friend was hanging from a large pentagram, blood running from his wrists and throat. He had been sacrificed! He looked as though he had been dead for hours. His skin was white, his lips had turned a pale blue.

They looked round the room to make sure no-one else was in it, and decided that they must try to get their friend out of there. As the room looked to be empty, they stepped inside.

In a basin to the side was a goat's head, surrounded by small candles, and on an altar to the left of them on the floor, another pentagram was drawn with mystical writing around it and a large candle on each of the points of the pentagram, with an open book laying in the very centre.

Sheets of red and black cloth hung from each of the walls surrounding the room, with the exception of a large ornate mirror on the right-hand wall, directly opposite the alter with the goat's head.

"We need to call the police." one of them whispered. At which point, their friend opened his eyes and groaned, which startled them and caused the girl to scream. They quickly tried to cover her mouth to silence her.

"Shhh, you'll give us away" one of the boys whispered. She was terrified though. She thought that she had just seen a dead man come back to life, and her heart was racing, panic setting in.

"We have to get him down, and quickly, if we can get him to a hospital, we might be able to save him." said the other boy, who began untying his feet to try get him down, the blood making his hands slip. 'c'mon, give me hand."

"Not me," whispered the girl, who was going into shock from the fright, shaking her head. "I just want to get out of here."

"THAT'S NOT GOING TO HAPPEN!"

Jennifer, who so far had been steadily making her voice quieter and quieter, to build both the tension to piano wire tautness, and the suspense to a nail-biting level, suddenly resumed in her normal, or slightly louder than normal, voice.

This had the desired effect of making both Jonathan and Elizabeth jump out of their proverbial skins.

"Oh, you arse!" said Elizabeth, slapping her arm. "You scared the life out of us."

Jennifer couldn't contain her amusement.

"Sorry, had to." she laughed.

"So? what happened?" asked Jonathan after a minute of calming down, still in the full grip of suspense.

"Well, in the struggle to get out, some of the candles got knocked over and set fire to the cloth draping from the walls. While the guys were fighting with the kidnappers, the girl helped the guy up the stairs and out to safety, but the four in the basement were overcome by the fumes and ended up burning to death. It's said that their ghosts still haunt the basement, the four of them trapped, forever engaged in a fight that will last all eternity". Jennifer finished off quickly.

"What a crock of shit," said Elizabeth "you were right about it not even scaring fourth graders. No-one's going to believe that nonsense."

"You were scared." retorted Jennifer, a little hurt.

"Only because you started shouting after talking so quiet. That's what made us jump, not that rubbish story." replied Elizabeth defensively.

Jonathan looked up at the shop front and shuddered. Something about the place gave him the creeps. Some part of the tale had obviously hooked into his psyche.

"Come on, let's have a look inside." Jennifer said, seeing Jonathan's shudder, and a hint of further mischievousness that was piquing inside her thought she could push a few more buttons and see if she could wind him up even further.

"Don't be silly," replied Jonathan "it's not even open, look there's no lights on."

"Sign on the door says it's open." said Jennifer, matter of factly and pointing at the sign. "Or are you scared?" and she leaned into his face, goading him.

Elizabeth, now cognizant of the wind up, could see what she was up to and decided to join in as well.

"Yeah, come on scaredy-cat. It's only a shop." and then, emulating a spooky tone of voice "What's the worst that could happen?" and with that she turned and pushed the door open.

A small bell tinkled to alert the shop owners they had custom.

The inside of the shop was very much in line with what its outside suggested. Low wattage bulbs gave off a faint orange hue of light that only seemed to permeate a few feet out into the room - hence the apparent darkness when observed from the outside. The shelves lined with a variety of strange objects, which, to Jonathan's mind, were overly stereotypical of second-hand shops, and played directly into the hands of the 'Aladdin's cave' persona that seemed to be synonymous with such shops.

'So much for window shopping' he thought to himself 'there is literally nothing in here I would consider buying for anyone. Well, not anyone I actually liked in any event'.

"C'mon, let's go." he said to Elizabeth & Jennifer "There's nothing in here."

"You have only been in for one minute. You could not possibly have seen everything in order to make such a claim." came a voice from somewhere within the shop.

The three of them stopped, slightly embarrassed, realising that they had been observed without them noticing. Even though they hadn't done anything particularly warranting embarrassment. They looked around trying to locate the source of the voice but could see no-one. After moving around a tall set of shelving they noticed, in a dark, dingy corner, a man sat at a wooden counter that had glass displays underneath, the kind that you might see in an early twentieth century sweet shop, although there were no sweets in this display, just an assortment of bohemian style rings, necklaces and other small trinkets.

They looked at the man for a few seconds. He looked vaguely familiar, but Jonathan couldn't place where he thought he might have seen him. He looked to be to be of average size and average build, although, being sat down and dressed in black in the dim light of the shop, his eyes could quite well be deceiving him. He appeared to be quite small, yet simultaneously, also appeared to occupy that whole corner of the shop, such was the effect of his black garments against the background in this dim light. The main discernible characteristics that stood out were, firstly, a long black beard that, in spite of the dullness of light in the shop, appeared to shine in a way that gave it the illusion of generating its own light source. The healthy appearance of it seemed at odds with the rest of the shop, which looked dusty, rusty and dull.

The next unusual characteristic of the man was his skin, which was an ill looking combination of pinkish-yellowy-brown and looked as though a jaundiced man had spent a great deal of time in the sun, even though they doubted he ever left the dim light of the shop. This made him look as though he were anywhere from forty to a hundred and forty years old.

The final item of unusualness about the man, was his clothing. To Jonathan, it reminded him of how a goth cowboy might look. A black cowboy hat, black shirt, black leather waistcoat and a black druids cape over the top.

The idea of a goth cowboy tickled him, and he struggled to keep from laughing at the idea.

"Yes, you're quite right." Jonathan replied, attempting to style it out. "I'm sorry."

The man didn't reply.

"We were just trying to get some ideas for Christmas gift." Elizabeth said, breaking the silence.

The man looked at them, with empty eyes, for a moment, and then the faintest of smiles flickered across his face, as though a pleasant memory had come to him that pleased him.

"Feel free to peruse at your leisure, I have many pagan relics that might suit your needs." he said finally. Signalling, with a broad sweep of his arm, the contents of the entire shop. He then returned his attention to something below the level of the counter.

Jonathan, Elizabeth and Jennifer exchanged a glance that said they had all drawn the same conclusion over the strangeness of the man and returned their attention back to the items on the shelves. They stayed huddled together so they might keep their conversation to just the three of them.

"There's nothing here that I would buy for anyone." Jonathan whispered as quietly as he could. "Look at it, it's all just dusty old tat!"

"Don't be mean." Elizabeth whispered back, in equally hushed tones. "It's not that bad, and you can usually find some real bargains in places like this."

"Bargains!? Look at this stuff. A creepy old doll with one eye. A child's toy that looks like it's from medieval times, a stone with glass buried in it and rusty old cutlery and tea trays! I mean, who on earth wants to buy second hand cutlery?"

Elizabeth nudged him with her elbow and held a finger to her lips to remind him to quieten down. His whispers were increasing in volume the more disgusted he became.

"It's gross!" he replied. Finally returning to a level somewhere between mouthing the words and whispering them.

"Look at these, guys" said Jennifer behind them. They turned to see what she was looking at. She had found a shelf full of antiquarian books. The looked at some of the titles 'The Revelations of St John the Divine', 'The Witches Bible', 'The Encyclopaedia of Demonology'.

"Wooooohhooohohohooho!!" whispered Jennifer in a mock ghostly tone, waving her hands in their faces.

"Give up, you idiot." said Elizabeth "Neither of us are scared by your silly story."

Jennifer giggled, clearly now the only one of them still amused by her antics.

Jonathan nudged Elizabeth. He had made his way round the corner and was looking up at the shelves on the opposite side of the shop.

"You may be right after all." he said, still whispering. "That silver tea tray looks like it could be cleaned up to look new, and it's just the sort of thing my gran would like. She loves those old ornate tea trays."

"See!" replied Elizabeth "You just have to look properly. Shops like these can be real treasure troves if you just look carefully enough."

"I know what I'm buying Jonathan." whispered Jennifer to them, and pointed a little way further down the same shelf.

They looked where she was pointing. Further down the shelf there was what looked like a cross between a gravy boat and a small copper kettle. It was dusty and cobwebbed, much like most of the items in the rest of the shop, and it looked as though it had been buried in ash and rubble for a long time before someone had retrieved it, given it a quick wipe over to 'clear the worst off' and then put it on the shelf, with a string price tag, to be ignored for several more years.

"It's Aladdin's lamp." joked Jennifer. "I'm going to buy it for you so you can polish it up and it will make all your dreams come true."

Jonathan smiled sarcastically back at her as she passed him the little trinket.

"I wish!" said Jonathan, attempting to join in the joke. "But I don't think two dollars is going to buy very many dreams." and he showed her the price tag.

"See! Treasure trove of bargains." she replied still in a hushed whisper glancing over to Elizabeth. "Okay, so you might need to use a bit of imagination." returning her attention to Jonathan.

"I see you found something after all," said the shop owner from the corner. "Maybe not all worthless old tat, eh?"

The three of them froze. There was no way he could possibly have heard their conversation. Not from the opposite end of the shop, and not considering how quietly they had spoken. They had barely even been able to hear each other, after all.

Jennifer approached the counter gingerly, her confidence not quite what it had been ten or fifteen minutes earlier. Maybe he could read minds or something, and that's how he had known what they were saying?

She told herself to stop being so silly, she was starting to get spooked by her own story, and she knew she had embellished it.

She paid the two dollars, and they left the shop as rapidly as they could.

The shopkeeper quietly returned to his book, his lips moving as he read something from within.

"Well, he was creepy." said Jennifer when they were safely outside.

"I'll say." said Jonathan, finally allowing himself to breath out. He hadn't been conscious of it, but he had been holding his breath since Jennifer had approached the counter. "And who's silly idea was it to go in in the first place?"

"Alright, alright! Bad idea. I'll admit. It's not like we ever have to go back in though, right?!"

"I've no intention of." replied Jonathan definitively.

"Me neither." agreed Elizabeth.

"It's pretty dark don't you think? what time is it?" asked Jonathan, suddenly noticing the blackness of the night.

"Half past six!" replied Jennifer with some surprise. "That can't be right!? We've never been in there for three hours!?" she continued incredulously.

Elizabeth and Jonathan checked their watches. They both read the same time.

"We were only in there fifteen minutes, tops." said Elizabeth, now feeling a little scared. They had lost a sizable chunk of time.

They looked at each other, each sharing the same sense of unease.

Chapter IV

Back at his apartment, Jonathan gave his first Christmas gift of the year a wipe over with a cloth, which didn't seem to make the slightest difference to its appearance. So, he dumped it on a shelf until he got chance to get to a Home Depot or DIY store so that he might buy some Brasso. It might be the only time he ever cleaned the thing, but he knew Jennifer would be looking for it the next time she visited so he had to at least give some semblance of caring about it. He could then move it somewhere out of sight knowing she'd also forget about it, after which he could palm it off to some other second-hand shop, or give it someone else as a gift. Not that he thought anyone would appreciate it. He would more likely send it to the dump.

He grabbed his study notes and went out. They'd arranged to meet at their apartment to study and he wanted to get there before they started without him.

They were always doing things like that - making arrangements knowing he was on the other side of the apartment block. They would start without him, then laugh at how flustered he got trying to find where they had got to. They only did it because they knew it wound him up, and it really did annoy him. He wished he had more control of himself so that he could suppress his reaction. He knew they'd stop if he didn't react. They would soon lose interest if he did, and it would make his life a lot easier.

In the elevator, on the way down to go meet them, he felt his stomach growling. He hadn't had anything to eat since around noon and realised just how ravenously hungry he was. He briefly contemplated going back to his apartment to make himself something, but a quick look at his watch told him it was already just past seven o'clock and he'd lose too much time if he went back. They would probably have already started as it was. They'd arranged to meet at seven and they would have a field day making fun of him for not being able to figure out where they had gotten up to.

He decided it would be easier to grab a quick burger from the fast-food restaurant, it was already on the way, and it would only take him a few minutes to go in and grab something that would put him on until after the study session; after which, they usually went out for something to eat anyway.

The restaurant was relatively empty, maybe a dozen people in all, separated into four or five separate groups.

One of the groups, off to his left, were students whose faces he vaguely recalled seeing around the campus, but whom he had never met or spoken to. Sat to the right of him were a group of four of the University football team, who were easily recognisable due to the team jackets they were wearing, like a uniform. He also noticed that they all looked in his direction. If there had been music playing, he felt sure it would have stopped, just like in the old western movies.

He tried to ignore them as best he could, but he felt an unnerving sense of foreboding when they began muttering and sniggering amongst themselves.

The girls stood in front of him at the counter seemed to be taking an age deciding what they wanted. Even as he had entered, they had been stood staring up at the menu board deciding, and they were still doing the same now.

He stared at the back of their heads willing them to hurry up and make a decision.

"Hey, slaphead!" one of the jocks called out. Jonathan kept his eyes firmly fixed at the back of the girl's heads, ignoring them, vainly hoping that he could simultaneously get them to hurry up, whilst also willing the jocks to ignore him and leave him in peace.

"Hey, slaphead! I'm talking to you." the jock called again.

Jonathan heard his friends laughing along now. Herd instincts kicking in. They were progressing from bored students trying to have a laugh, to a pack of wild hyenas, calling out that they had identified prey and were about to move in. He knew he didn't have long; he'd been in this type of situation too many times before.

His eyes darted around the restaurant, instinctively, wondering who, if anyone, might come to his aid. The group to his left had stopped their own conversation and had turned their attention to the situation unfolding here, eyes skipping between him at the counter, and the jocks, fifteen feet further away, in their booth. They sensed what was happening, but would they help him? or goad the jocks on?

The girls in front of him seemed oblivious, quietly talking to each other. They seemed to have decided what to order at least.

"Two cheeseburgers and two diet cokes." they said to the lady behind the counter, a blond-haired lady who looked as though she could be as young as mid-thirties and as old as mid-fifties depending entirely on what light she was stood in. She was stood looking directly at them, allowing them a second or two to remember their manners, but thought better of pushing the point after catching a glimpse of Jonathan's nervously fearful looking face. Instead, she just rolled her eyes in contempt at them taking so long to decide on such a simple, and cheap, order.

"He's ignoring you, man," one of the jocks friends said "disrespecting you, bro. You should do something; you can't let a nerd disrespect you."

"Hey nerd! Slaphead! Look at me when I'm talking to you! the jock called out, beginning to get more agitated. His friends' comments were needling away at his ego which in turn was becoming inflamed. He didn't want to lose face in front of his friends.

The girls, whose attention was no longer focused on the menu, turned to look at the jocks, then to Jonathan, and then back to the jocks, as though they had only just noticed that any of them existed, and they were struggling to piece the situation together, and whether or not it involved them.

As Jonathan stepped up to the counter, the lady behind it placed a cheeseburger and cardboard container of fries on the counter and in a quietened voice said.

"Cheeseburger and fries do ya, hun? I'm guessing the quicker the better, right?" and she gave a quick glance - a glance that contained within it an entire conversation, that, not only did she understand what was going on, but that she had seen this kind of thing before with bullies. That she felt nothing but compassion for him, and the best way she could help was to serve him as quickly as she could so he could get out of there as fast as humanly possible - and tipped her head in the direction of the booth where the jocks were sat.

"Yes, thank you." Jonathan muttered back, passing the money quickly before turning to leave.

He didn't want to rush out too quickly. If he showed too much urgency then the pack of hyenas would sense it, and move in for the kill; but, in the same vein, he certainly didn't want to hang around for even one second longer than was necessary.

He gathered his burger and fries and turned to make his way towards the exit, his heart now beating in his ears; caused by the vast amount of adrenalin surging through his veins along with the nervousness he felt being in this kind of situation again. His appetite had gone, and he was sorely tempted to leave his order behind, but, he figured, the time it would take to turn around and put it back on the countertop could be valuable time, and so huddled them into his midriff and stepped forward, as calmly and casually as he could, given his predicament, but also as briskly as he could muster.

He had only taken two paces when he heard movement off to his left, and, despite knowing already that it was the jocks moving, he couldn't help but cast a fast glance in their direction. The one that had been harassing him had stood up, chest puffed out in some animalistic display of dominance, and was looking around to see if anyone else wanted to disrespect him. No one did. What they did do, however, was watch him carefully to see what was going to happen next. He looked silly, standing there, chest pushed out like some kind of gorilla, but they had expectations, there were fights on campus all the time, and they wanted their entertainment. They just wanted to make sure that they didn't become the entertainment themselves.

Jonathan kept moving towards to door. He was only four or five paces away, but the knowledge that the jocks had begun to move on him caused an odd sensation to come over him. Time seemed to slow; he became hyper aware of everything around him. He'd heard that flies have a sense of time akin to what he was now experiencing. That they were hyper aware of everything around them and that was why they could react so quickly. He also found it bizarre that, at a time when he felt extreme fear for his physical wellbeing, it should be flies that he was thinking of. The salty smell of fries, fatty beefburgers, the scent of the girls' perfume, the distance to the door, how long it would take him to get to it, and through it. How far away the jocks were, how long it would take them to close the gap, even accounting for them moving faster than he could. Three paces now for him, seven for them; he should be able to get to the door and through it before they did, but he'd only have a couple of paces advantage, so he'd have to yank the door closed behind him and start running immediately; then pray that they deemed him of insufficient significance for them to pursue further, because if they did, he would be caught in less than twenty yards. It was all down to fate.

By the time he got to Elizabeth and Jennifers apartment block he was drastically out of breath and sweating. His burger was an amorphous blob, and he had lost more than half of the box of fries; not that he was bothered as his appetite was even less than it had been at the restaurant a few minutes earlier, but at least the jocks hadn't made too much of an effort to chase him. All it had amounted to was them running, half-heartedly, a few yards - just enough to save face - and laughing at him, shouting further insults at him from a few yards away from the doorway.

He sat on the low wall outside the apartment block and took off his jacket so that he might cool down and let the sweat dry off before he went in to join Elizabeth and Jennifer for the study session.

He put the half destroyed wax paper wrapped burger, and the three-quarter empty cardboard box of fries on the wall beside him and let his head hang. Right there, right then, he felt about as lonely as he had ever felt in his life. He hated his looks, hated his hair, or lack of, and, more than anything, he hated his life. Even before his thinning hair cursed him, he wasn't exactly the most popular person in school, but at least people let him be. But since, it was as though his odd appearance drew people's attention and made them feel like they had the right to mock him. They no longer ignored him. No! now they were targeting him. Oh, to be ignored once more!

He'd lost all enthusiasm for studying, all he wanted to do was go back to his apartment, turn off the lights, get under to covers and let an eternal sleep wash over him.

He managed to push those thoughts to one side and, after settling his breathing, got up and went up to the study group they had arranged.

* * * *

That night Jonathan tossed and turned in his bed. He hated nights like this. His body throbbed from the exertions of the day, but he was also restless. Thinking about it, he had overdone things. A full day of lectures, walking all over the campus, then walking into town to meet Jennifer and Elizabeth. Then, the three of them had walked back, and then, after their study group, they had all walked back into town for something to eat and then walked back again. He had done some miles, that was for sure, and now he was suffering the consequences. He was exhausted. Or rather, his body was exhausted, but his mind would not stop. Thoughts were bouncing around his head like a squash ball on court mid match - things his lecturers had said that he couldn't remember if he'd made notes on and whether it would come up in an exam. The weird way the shop owner spoke. The snide comments from the jocks in the take-away. Why they had walked so far today. The superhuman hearing of the shop owner and the way he could hear them from the other side of the shop even though they could barely hear each other stood next to one another. Jennifers silly ghost Story. What he should have said to those Jocks instead of being scared and staying quiet, letting them get away without retort.

He was driving himself mad. He needed to focus his mind on something else.

Getting out of bed, he switched on his desk lamp and quickly jotted down his recollections of what the lecturer had said - he could cross reference his other notes later, and if he had already made the notes, he could easily discard these ones but at least he would have them. He also wrote down the snide remarks the jocks had made and included some of the retorts that he could think of; these made him smile to himself. 'If only I had the confidence to have said these at the time' he thought.

Once this was done, he made himself a hot cup of drinking chocolate whilst he ran himself a bath. It was an old trick his grandmother had taught him. "If you can't sleep at night," she said. "Have a hot bath and a warm drink. It takes the blood from your brain that's causing you to overthink, down to your stomach and body so you feel drowsy."

He wasn't certain of her rationale, but ninety-nine times out of a hundred that he had tried this it had worked for him, so he didn't really care.

He drank the chocolate and climbed into the bath. The water was hot, but bearable. Just. He lowered himself in slowly, and submerged himself as much as he could.

He found it odd that baths were never quite big enough. If he kept his legs straight, half his torso was out of the water, or, if he submerged his torso, then his legs would be sticking out like chopstick from a bowl of rice. If *he* owned a bath company, he'd make them long enough to lie in completely. He was sure it would make him a fortune.

He sat in the hot bath contemplating being a wealthy bath magnate.

The hot water gently lapped over his skin turning it a vibrant shade of pink as the blood rose to the surface. He slid down, submerging his stomach and chest and let his rosy legs slide out of the bottom of the tub. He had already forgotten all about the things that had been keeping him awake and felt so relaxed that he wasn't sure he'd be able to get out. He had to admit, the older generations knew a thing or two.

After a few minutes he felt his eyes getting heavy, and a drowsiness washing over him. 'Don't want to fall asleep in the bath and wake up with pneumonia' he thought to himself, so he grabbed the bar of soap, gave himself a quick once over, making sure to wash the sweat off his head, and pulled the plug out. He stood for a few seconds watching the bathwater flow down the plughole. He was feeling very drowsy now, the hot chocolate and bath having the desired effect. He dried himself lazily, but as quickly as he could so he could get back into bed. His dreams that night were filled with his encounter with the jocks.

* * * *

He woke feeling much more refreshed. The echoes of his strange dream still hazily present in his mind, but by the time he had showered and had his breakfast - buttered toast and coffee - they had quite slipped away.

His walk to university that morning was a pleasant one. The air cold and crisp. Fresh, as you would expect in late autumn. The sun shone in a clear blue sky, which left a vague uneasy sensation brewing away deep in his mind. He felt as though he had already walked this exact same journey. The sky, the cool freshness of the air, even the clothes he was wearing all felt overly familiar. He shook it off, as he had walked this route for the past year and this wasn't the first time he had worn these clothes, nor felt the clean crispness of the air. He figured that his mind had taken on these external stimuli and merged them together into one meta-feeling. He saw Elizabeth and Jennifer up ahead in the University atrium and forgot all about it.

"Hi, you okay?" he asked them.

"Yeah." they replied in unison, unenthusiastically.

"What's up?"

"Just tired." replied Jennifer. "Last night took it out of me."

"Me too," said Elizabeth. "And I couldn't sleep last night either. I kept thinking about that creepy shop owner."

"Really? got a bit of a crush on him, have you?" Joked Jennifer laughing.

"Eeyeww! no way." replied Elizabeth firmly, pulling a face "He looked awful. His skin was a weird colour, like he was sick or something. And what about that freaky hearing he had!? how he could he hear us whispering from across the shop I do not know. I could hardly hear you guys, and we were stood next to each other. It was weird. Totally creeped me out. I'm never going back in there again, that's for sure."

"You'll not get any arguments from me," said Jonathan. "I didn't want to go in in the first place."

"You guys are so lame! We were only window shopping. Nothing ventured, nothing gained, right?" replied Jennifer.

"Nothing ventured?" replied Elizabeth "we lost hours of time. How do you explain that?"

Jennifer shrugged.

"Whatever," said Jonathan "the lecture starts in a minute, c'mon we'd best get in".

They rushed across the atrium, down the corridor and into the lecture hall, which was completely empty. This was the first time they had been the first students in, and as there were no other students behind them, they had to double check that they had the right day and time.

"Have we got the right day?" Elizabeth asked, confused.

"Yeah, Thursday morning 10 a.m., Social Psychology with Professor Malim." replied Jennifer, still a little unsure. "We must just be a bit early. Come on, we've got the pick of seats, let's grab these three on the front row."

Jonathan halted for a brief second.

"Woah, that's spooky." he said as they made their way forward "but I totally knew you were going to say that."

"Great minds, eh!? Best view, fewer distractions and quickest to leave afterwards." she replied tapping her temple.

Jonathan sat in silence a moment.

"I knew you were going to say that too."

"Do you know what Professor Malim is going to say in his lecture as well? coz if you do, we don't need to sit here for the next hour and a half. We can go back to our apartment, write up our notes and have an extra hour's rest".

Jonathan gave a sarcastic smirk, but in his mind, he wondered if he actually might. Everything else about the day so far had a semblance of Deja vu to it.

"Very funny. I was just saying."

At that point the other students began to enter the hall and take their seats. The normal bustle and chatter enveloped the three of them and Jonathan's uneasiness subsided.

Ninety minutes later, their lecture ended, and they packed up their papers and made their way out.

"Did you guys get any decent notes?" Elizabeth asked.

"Yeah, more or less, why?" asked Jennifer.

"I couldn't concentrate in there. I'm so tired, I kept nodding off. Can I borrow your notes so I can write them up?

"I've got to do some work on them first, but yeah, sure. You owe me though."

"Done. Come on, let's go grab a coffee and we can get started."

They spent the next hour or so huddled in the corner of a coffee shop making notes and discussing the lecture.

"I need something to eat, I'm starving" said Jennifer eventually. "Come on, we'll pick up something and go back to ours. We can pick up where we left off when we've eaten."

"Yeah, good call," said Jonathan "these seats aren't exactly the most comfortable either." and with that they collected their belongings and made their way back.

A few minutes later they came up to a burger bar, inside which were the same Jocks that he had encountered before. Just their luck. As soon as the Jocks saw him, they began heckling him, picking up from where they had left off previously.

"Hey look," said a large blond-haired jock, who seemed to be the ringleader "it's the nerd turds again."

"Ignore him." whispered Elizabeth to Jonathan

"Easier said than done." replied Jonathan.

"Hey nerd turd. You out with your bitches?" shouted the jock, whose name was Josh, laughing and signalling to his friends to do likewise, to which they duly obliged, compounding the ridicule.

Jonathan scowled at them in return.

"It takes one to know one." replied Jonathan, with more aggression than he knew he had.

"Woah!" came the collective response from almost everyone in the immediate vicinity. It was a rare occurrence that anyone spoke up to the jocks, and even more alarming that it was Jonathan, of all people.

"What'd you say nerd turd?" came an aggressive reply.

"I called you a bitch. Or are you deaf as well as dumb?"

"Jonathan, what are you doing?" whispered Elizabeth into his ear, desperately. She had no idea what has come over him and knew it would end badly. Josh just stood there silently. He wasn't accustomed to people talking back to him and it took him a moment to process the information.

Jonathan was sick of always getting bullied, he felt it was about time he stood up for himself, and, if he got beaten up, then he had at least said something that warranted it for once. Normally, he just got beaten up for no reason.

"Well," said Jonathan, after a moments silence "are you a bitch? you got no dick? come on, show everyone your tiny dick."

Everyone burst out laughing at how ridiculous this had become. Josh, thinking everyone was now laughing at him, frantically began looking around for support, but everywhere he looked he just saw faces laughing. He'd always been proud of his manhood, so he thought 'why not' it'll shut everyone up. He undid his pants and showed them. However, instead of his usual sized manhood that he was used to seeing, he had revealed something less than half the size.

Elizabeth and Jennifer brought their hands up to cover their mouths but couldn't supress their laughter. Josh could not understand what was happening and how this came to be. All his friends were pointing and laughing hysterically, in his face.

Josh's embarrassment was spectacular.

He looked Jonathan square in the face, his fury evident to all.

"You! ... You've done something! ... What have you done?"

Jonathan held his hands up in innocence, but he joined in the ridiculing laughter.

Josh could not stand this. His anger and rage welled up inside him and escalated to bursting point in a matter of seconds. He rushed towards Jonathan, the sole target of all his rage.

Jonathan noticed, and immediate regret washed over him. He turned to run away, but no matter how hard he tried, he just could not move. He felt like he was trying to run through a river of treacle, his effort insufficient to gain him any movement, and it seemed to cause his joints pain. It was like his legs were suddenly made of lead and he just completely lacked the strength to even so much as lift a knee to move them.

Josh collided into the back of him, knocking him to the ground, turned him over and began punching him in the face, beating him relentlessly, busting his nose and his lip, his eyes quickly swelling to a close from the bruising.

It wasn't until what seemed like an age later that he heard Jennifer and Elizabeth screaming, and the beating subsided, and he felt Josh get dragged off him. He lay there, still. Despite the heavy beating he had just taken. He realised he had barely felt any of it. He was certainly aware he was being hit, he could see the fists coming at his face, but at the moment of contact, he could neither see, nor feel, anything. He felt the after-effects though, which was mildly upsetting.

Josh, noticing that Jonathan was lying there motionless and, thinking he had killed him, ran off, along with his friends.

He hadn't been killed, of course. But he did feel dazed and on the brink of unconsciousness, so felt he should lay still as he gathered his senses.

He carried out a mental scan of where he hurt, and how badly. And, though in tremendous pain, he concluded that nothing too severe was the matter with him, allowed his awareness to permeate further out, into his surroundings. He became aware that both Elizabeth and Jennifer were crouched over him in a mixture of concern over his well-being, that bordered on mothering, and fawning over him, telling him how brave they thought he was standing up to the bullies like that.

Elizabeth caressed him delicately and he noticed Jennifer seemed to be flickering her eyelashes at him. This was entirely out of character for Jennifer, who's usual demeanour was naturally one of sarcastic mockery.

He looked up into Jennifers eyes again, in case he was imagining it all, or if he was hallucinating due to concussion, or some brain trauma that he might have received in the attack. He noticed she had stopped flickering her eyelashes and was back to her normal demeanour once again, looking at him as though he were completely stupid and that she was so horrendously disappointed in him that she struggled to find the words.

Elizabeth had also stopped her fawning and caressing and merely had her hands under his arm trying to help him to get up.

Maybe he had just been hallucinating?

Together, they helped him back to his feet and walked with him back to his apartment to get cleaned up.

Upon leaving Elizabeth paused at his door, turned and said,

"See you later, hot stuff." gave a seductive wink, ran her tongue over her lips, suggestively, and closed the door behind her.

Jonathan sat with his eyes and mouth wide open, staring at the closed door.

He spent the rest of the evening turning over in his mind the way both Jennifer and Elizabeth had behaved, and what it all meant.

Was he suffering from concussion and his mind playing tricks? Were their feelings towards him changing due to his encounter with Josh. They had said how brave they thought he was, after all. Did women really fall for men who had been beaten mercilessly? He'd always been under the belief that it was the stronger, victorious men who garnered women's favour? Maybe that was just in romance novels and movies? Maybe they just pitied him and would resume their normal behaviour in a day or so, once things had time to be forgotten.

He fell asleep with his mind full of fanciful encounters with them and, as a result, had some rather lucid dreams of romantic liaisons, which, thankfully, took his mind off the bruises and swelling on his face as well as the, currently unthought of, fact that he would bump into Josh again and he may just take it on himself to continue their recent encounter.

Chapter V

The next morning Jonathan woke with his head still swimming from the nocturnal theatre that had been performing in his head, and it brought a smile to his lips. His lips then reminded him that they were both swollen and had been split, via an acute pain from the scab which had formed on his bottom lip, popping open, which soon wiped the smile from his face.

Still, it started his day with him being in a good mood. This, too, was quickly changed when he observed himself in the mirror of his small bathroom.

He gazed at the unrecognizable image that reflected back at him. His nose had a small scar running horizontally across the bridge which indicated it had been broken by at least one of Josh's heavy blows, although, on closer inspection it appeared that the break was not displaced, which was only a small mercy.

Both his eyes were shadowed with a purple bruising underneath, this faded to a greenish yellow at the extremities. His eyes were puffy with swelling, his left eye more so, and he could feel the heaviness of it around the socket.

It didn't look good, and he didn't want to think about how much worse it would have looked had he not had a bag of frozen peas held to it at intervals throughout the previous evening.

He filled the sink with warm water, gingerly wiping the crusted blood from his nose and lip, which was so swollen it looked as though a prosthetic lip had been poorly glued in its place. Had it not felt like he had a throbbing water balloon for a lip, he would have been inclined to try remove it.

Once cleaned up he made his way to the kitchen to seek out the frozen peas once again. He wanted, nay needed, to reduce some more of the swelling so that he might be in a position to be able to try and have something to eat; he was remarkably hungry after the previous day's exertions.

He made himself comfortable on the couch, with the peas held to his mouth, and contemplated what he should do. He didn't want to go outside looking like this, but he also had no intentions of falling behind in his studies, he had worked far too hard to get here to let that happen. He grabbed his diary and flipped through the pages.

Realising that he didn't even know what day it was he checked his phone. Friday. He revisited the diary, no lectures today. A wave of relief brushed over him and he immediately relaxed knowing that he could stay at home without further worry, and focus on getting his face back to a state of presentability.

He was just at the point of the peas no longer being frozen when he heard a gentle knocking on his door.

He sighed. He really wasn't in any mood for visitors, not whilst he looked like this.

"Hew iff ith?" he called out. His fat lips preventing him from speaking any more coherently.

"It's Elizabeth." came a hushed reply from the other side of the door. The sound of her voice gave echoes back to the sultry tone in which she had spoken to him the previous evening, but he didn't let the thought linger, giving his head a shake, realising she was speaking through a door and trying to do so quietly enough to not arouse any interest from the rest of the floor.

He got up and went to open the door.

The first thing he noticed was the long beige trench coat that she was wearing. He was also vaguely aware she had bright red lipstick on, and her hair was down, wavy, full bodied, gleaming almost, and covering more than half her face, but he was so confused by her wearing a trench coat that he didn't bother to take any more notice about the rest of her face. He also saw she was wearing highly polished shiny black stilettos.

This proved even more confusing. Elizabeth never wore anything like this. She was very much a 'Plain Jane' looking girl ordinarily. Jeans, T-shirts and canvas trainers. Comfort was her forte. This was a far cry from that.

"How's the patient today?" she asked, pushing him back into the room and flicking the door shut behind her.

He blinked a few times, completely caught off guard by her appearance. Then he got a hold of himself.

"A bith bruithed, but owl liff" he replied.

"Maybe you need a nurse's attention!?" she replied, and before he could say a word, or even ask what on earth she was talking about, she undid the trench coat, pushed Jonathan back, one handed, until he reached the armchair, falling backwards into its welcoming arms.

Jonathan did a double take, blinking hard several times, almost cartoon like.

She was stood before him in lacy underwear, stockings and suspenders. Like something from an adult movie.

"Oh, it looks like I forgot my uniform," she said in feigned surprise. "I am a naughty nurse. I guess I'll have to be disciplined!" and with that, she turned and bent over, provocatively, to pick up the coat. Her thong clad buttocks only inches away from his face. She turned to look over her shoulder.

"Well?"

Jonathan was utterly speechless, his brain was doing cartwheels, flipping over and over itself, trying to comprehend what was occurring right before his very eyes. He couldn't concentrate. But she had achieved the result he thought she was trying to achieve. Nothing had ever aroused his interest to such an extent before in his whole life.

Seeing he was about as animated as a rabbit caught in a car's headlights, she slapped her behind and then sat back into his lap, giggling coquettishly.

"Oh, you are pleased to see me." she said, suggestively, and leaned back into his lap, resting her head against his shoulder. He couldn't help his gaze falling to her cleavage. She took hold of both his hands and used them to caress her body, guiding them down between her legs letting off a fake moan of pleasure.

After a few seconds, she quickly spun round, took off his trousers and made love to him in the chair. All the while Jonathan's mind raced with confusion over how all this had come to happen.

Ten minutes after she had finished and left Jonathan's apartment, he was still sat in the chair in a state of shock, and still trying to process what had happened. All he could think of was the shoes, the lipstick, the trench coat, and what lay underneath it. For the life of him, he couldn't remember a single thing of her face. Her eyes, nose, cheeks. All came back blank, as though she were a faceless body.

For about half an hour, he also completely forgot about the pulsating pain, bruising, and general state of his own face.

* * * *

It was the other side of the weekend, and numerous applications of the frozen peas, before the swelling of his face had abated, and the deeper purple bruises had faded to a pinker greenish-yellow colour. The scars were still clearly visible, but he'd had enough time to come to terms with their presence for him to be okay at the thought of going out into the world again. Plus, he rationalised, the campus gossip would have spread word of what had happened by now. The fact that he had only been visited once, told him that, either no-one cared, or, that they were uncomfortable about seeing him and talking about it. He doubted the latter was the case. These were students, after all, and they loved nothing more than gossiping about what everyone else was doing. This left him with the 'no-one cares' option, and in which case if they didn't care, then neither should he.

The lecture he was in that day was the same lecture Jennifer and Elizabeth were in, so he decided to go round to their apartment first. Their reaction would be a useful indicator of how the rest of the student body would respond. Not that he was a little paranoid, but he was. He felt he would have a little more confident having a couple of friends with him the first time he went back to the campus. Plus, he wanted to see Elizabeth again. He smiled at the thought.

It was Jennifer who answered the door.

"Oh my god!" she cried the moment she saw him. "What happened to your face?"

Elizabeth appeared behind her, hearing the alarm in Jennifers voice.

"Jesus Jonathan! what the hell happened to you?" Elizabeth echoed.

Jonathan was surprised by their response, and the apparent genuineness of their appeals. Were they winding him up?

"Well, you should have seen the other guy" he joked along.

"You've been in a fight?!" they exclaimed, in unison. "Who with?"

Jonathan regarded them both suspiciously. He couldn't tell if they were still on the wind up. They had been with him when he was beaten, yet, here they were, acting like this was the first time they had seen him. The alarm in their voices appeared to be genuine and he was, for a moment, lost for words. A silent "wha?" forming on his lips. They were being so sincere.

"Very funny." has said, finally, deciding they were winding him up.

"There's nothing funny about the state of your face, Jonathan" replied Jennifer, pointedly. "What happened? Come on, you know you can trust us."

"You were both there," he half said, half questioned "C'mon guys, quit messing. I'm okay about it, really."

Jennifer looked back at Elizabeth questioningly. Elizabeth shrugged.

"What are you talking about 'we were there'." asked Jennifer.

Jonathan was starting to get a little tired with their games, so thought he'd be better off getting them to admit to it so that they could all get back to being normal again.

"At my apartment, when I tripped and smashed my head on the kitchen surface." he said, a little too sarcastically.

Jennifer and Elizabeth looked at each other confused.

"We haven't been to your apartment in weeks," said Elizabeth.

"Thats right." said Jennifer "In fact we haven't even seen you since the lecture on Thursday. Where have you been? We were supposed to meet up to study, but you didn't show," she paused for a moment, uncertain of what she was saying, and then turned to Elizabeth to clarify "Did we study on Thursday? I don't remember?"

Elizabeth opened her mouth to speak, then thinking hard, and failing to come up with anything, closed it again and thought some more.

"I don't remember, either." she replied, confusion etched across her face. "In fact, I don't remember much of Friday either, for that matter ... Oh my god! have we been roofied!?"

"Who by though?" asked Jennifer "There's been a dozen or so people in here."

"Not necessarily. We only need to think of people we were with after the lecture on Thursday, and Friday morning. We must have been roofied on Thursday, as that's the last thing we both remember. We just need to make a list of everyone we spent time with on Thursday afternoon," replied Elizabeth "and honestly, we have to suspect everyone!"

"Oh my god!" replied Jennifer, in disbelief " I can't believe someone we know has drugged us."

Jonathan stood listening to them, in silence, for the next ten minutes as their paranoia grew. Any vague idea that he may still have had that they were leading him on about pretending not to remember, had now evaporated from his mind. He ran through the chain of events. His encounter with Josh, Jennifer and Elizabeth positively fawning over him as he lay on the floor bleeding, Elizabeth, or someone who looked like a relative of hers, visiting his room the following morning. His unnerving feeling of Deja-vu, and the fact that neither of them appeared to have the faintest recollection of any of these events. Had they all been drugged, and they were each getting different snaps of memory of some weird trip they had been on? That would certainly explain his false sense of bravery. It might even explain his perception of their behaviour towards him. But then, he remembered more clearly that they did, and he wasn't missing any time like they were. It also didn't explain his strange sense of Deja-vu. Which wasn't just an obtuse sensation of remembrance, more an acute feeling of reliving time.

The more he thought, the more he could sense a voice at the back of his head, whispering to him, like a faint echo from far away, there, but not there at the same time. A secret his subconscious was attempting to relay, but his conscious mind was not ready to hear it yet. Either that, or the escalating paranoic conversation that Elizabeth and Jennifer were having was stopping him from thinking rationally, the noise blocking out his subconscious minds attempts to communicate with its conscious counterpart.

"I have to go." he said suddenly, and walked out of the room, leaving them to it. He needed peace and quiet to think, to get that niggly faint voice from the back of his head closer to the forefront so he could better determine what it was attempting to tell him.

He hated this feeling. It was the thought equivalent of being about to say something, only to find that what you were just about to say had completely slipped from your mind.

He wanted to think *something*...no, not 'wanted to think *something'* exactly, more like he had an idea that had taken a wrong turning somewhere along the neural network of his brain, from wherever it had originated, to where it was supposed to end up, and he was attempting to retrace those steps... In the dark...while blindfolded; and if he didn't solve this it would distract and frustrate him to the point of intellectual paralysis.

He got back to his room sometime later, put on his headphones to block out distractions from the outside world. He'd been really pleased at finding these headphones. He was sceptical about their noise cancelling ability at first, but the moment he first put them on he had been converted. Ordinary background noise - such as the hustle and bustle of activity out on the landing, or the noise of cars on the roads outside the apartment block - were completely obsolete. Even when someone was in the room talking directly to you, he struggled to hear them. He took a few controlled breaths to calm his nerves before he set to his task of focusing on what that voice in his head was saying. He kept replaying the chain of events through his mind, trying to coax the voice to the forefront.

Suddenly, it hit him.

The event with Josh, him ridiculing him and all Josh's friends laughing, Josh exposing himself and finding his manhood to be half sized. It was all exactly as had happened in a dream that he'd had. Josh beating him up and Elizabeth and Jennifer pitying him, uncharacteristically fawning over him. Another dream he'd had, Elizabeth's visit to his apartment, although not Elizabeth, as, though she had claimed that to be her name, and he thought it sounded like her, the girl looked nothing like Elizabeth, now he thought about it. But still, exactly as had happened in another of his dreams.

All of these were his dreams being re-enacted in real life.

He shook his head at the preposterousness of what he was thinking. The very notion was ludicrous. And yet.

No. Peoples dreams do not come to life, that kind of thing only happens in Children's fairy tales. Still, he could not deny the fact that these things *were* happening to him, and they *were* all events that he had dreamed, quite vividly.

He was conflicted; His rational mind telling him that dreams, categorically, do not come true. His same rational mind reminded him, quite unequivocally, that these events had most definitely occurred, in objective reality, and that these events were the exact same events in those dreams.

His head began to spin. Could he trust his own mind to be reasonable? He needed to talk this out with someone. But who? How could he expect anyone to believe him? he could hardly believe himself. The people who he could talk to were all involved in these real-life dreamscapes and, seemingly, had no recollection.

They would think he had gone insane.

Instead, he decided that he should pay closer attention to the things that he had dreamt about at night, and see if any more of them came true. He made sure he had a pad and pen next to his bed, so that the first thing he would do was document what he had dreamed. Then he could reference against it anything that happened through the course of the following days.

He spent the next three or four nights making every conceivable attempt to dream. This proved far more difficult than he had thought, as, every morning, when he woke, he could not recall a single item of what he had dreamed that night. He needed to somehow make sure he dreamed. He wasn't sure how he could force himself to do so, or even if it were possible. It seemed the more he tried, the less he was able. He would have to try to figure out what it was that triggered dreaming. He cast his mind back to the first one he had had recently. The encounter with Josh and his gang of friends.

The night before this, he had dreamed that he had seen a couple of kids of around fifteen or sixteen, being bullied by a group of teenagers a year or so older. He had stood and watched them be bullied, unable to do anything about it. He had tried to call out, only to find that fear prevented any sound from leaving his mouth, strangling his vocal cords. He was completely mute. When he tried to move he found he was held fast, as though by some invisible spiders web; and so he had given up, just stood there in his dream, watching them being bullied mercilessly, partly wondering why he cared about a couple of complete strangers, and partly feeling a tremendous sadness and empathy for them, because he had been in exactly these kind of situations himself when he was their age. And, he was sad that he was as powerless now, as he had been back then, to do anything to prevent it from happening. His sadness and empathy turned into annoyance at himself.

In the dream, Josh - who he had no recollection of ever meeting before this point - had ridiculed him in a similar fashion, using the same insults as he had been taunted with as a child, but this time, he had stood up for himself.

This made him wonder. There had also been, within his dream, some latent sexual feelings for either Jennifer, or Elizabeth, or both, that he never knew he had, or maybe just refused to admit to himself. He let these slide from his focus and brought himself back to the ridiculing that had bothered him.

When he had first started University, he had noticed the looks he was given by other students due to his appearance. He resembled a teenager with the hair of a sixty-year-old monk. He knew it looked odd, but, much to his regret, he had waited a few weeks till after the half-whispered insults had already started before shaving it off. He'd wished he had had the foresight to shave it before he turned up to university, as these other students wouldn't have known him look any differently, had he done so.

As it was, he had turned up looking something akin to Benjamin Button, which then caused him to be the recipient of several comments, ranging from the 'less than complimentary' to the 'downright obscene'. This all meant that they had about a month of getting used to his old look, before he changed his appearance, which then gave them something else to comment about. It had taken him a long time to forget about the way he'd been treated, in some cases, he still bore a grudge. Only Elizabeth and Jennifer had never said anything really hurtful, although they had both had their opinions.

He sat, wishing he'd shaved it before he came to Uni, but then realised that he didn't wish that at all. He wished that he had never been bald in the first place. In fact, he wished he had long, silky flowing hair that came down the middle of his back.

He fell asleep dreaming of having long hair.

Chapter VI

Jonathan woke thick headed and groggy the next morning. He looked at the clock on the side table. Three minutes to ten. He had slept in.

Panic set in.

He grabbed a sweater and pair of jeans, bypassing his normal morning routine of a shower, and didn't bother to change his underwear from the day before either. He ran out of his apartment, trying not to be any later for his lecture than he knew he was about to be.

He arrived at the lecture hall seven minutes later. He doubted it was conceivably possible for anyone short of an Olympic athlete to have gotten there any quicker, and he paused a moment outside the door, taking in huge lungful's of air in an attempt to get himself into a reasonably presentable state.

Given the burning sensation he felt in his lungs, this took a little longer than he thought it might, and certainly more than he wanted to allow for. But, at the very least, he wanted the flush from his cheeks to dissipate. He wasn't naturally athletically inclined, so this, rather frustratingly, also took longer than he'd have liked. Conscious of missing any more of the lecture, he pushed the door open gently, still flushed, still trying to get a control of his breath, and trying to do so as quietly as he possibly could. He would have been considerably more successful in this, had his bag handle not caught on the handle of the door, crashing him back into it.

The whole auditorium stared at the strange red-faced man who was struggling to free himself from the door whilst huffing for breath. With as much decorum as he could muster, he freed himself from the door and tried to find a seat. At least people wouldn't be able to tell if he was just flushed from the physical exertion he had just undertaken, or if he was merely embarrassed. Neither of which were particularly preferred.

"Are you finished?" the lecturer asked him when he was finally sat down. Jonathan quietly raised a hand of apology, and the lecturer returned his attention back to the class.

"When it comes to aggression in any social conflict, Freud theorised that we each have two opposing instincts at play within us. One of self-preservation, and life, the other of Self destruction, and death. He called these two instincts Eros and Thanatos, respectively, from the Greek..."

Jonathan started at these words. The feeling of Deja-vu sparking in his conscious once again. This sounded exactly like the Social Psychology lecture they'd had the previous week. If that was true, then he should be sat in the centre of the front row with Elizabeth and Jennifer. He craned his head so as to get a better look.

There they were. Elizabeth looking as though she was nodding off, Jennifer bent over her notepad frantically taking notes. He opened his own notebook and there it was. Social Psychology, Professor Malim, with the date followed by the three pages of notes which he had taken. At the top of the first page he could see, in his own handwriting "conflict, Freud. Eros & Thanatos - further reading." to remind himself to look these up after the lecture.

This was very unnerving. Had he dreamed this? He had no recollection of it. He thought hard, trying to resurrect his dream from the previous night. He'd been in such a rush due to sleeping in that he hadn't had time to think about it, nor write anything down while he'd still had any of it fresh in his mind. All he could recall of it was him having long hair. Any details were hazy, like trying to see distant figures through fog, or looking at a Turner painting too close up, only a vague hint of what you were looking at being evident, forcing you to look harder and concentrate more in order to see, leaving it up to the mind to try fill in the gaps, except his mind wasn't filling them in.

Suddenly he snapped back, very self-aware; if he'd dreamed of having hair, did that mean he now had hair? He had best check himself to see if this had also happened. He slowly raised his hand to his head to scratch his scalp. Still bald. No full head of hair as he had thought he'd dreamed. He gave a deliberately controlled sigh of relief. He had no idea how he'd be able to explain being bald the previous day and now, suddenly, having a full head of the stuff.

Something else must be going on. Why was he reliving last week's lecture? What else could he have dreamed that would account for it?

As he already had notes from this lecture, he decided to focus his thoughts on what he could see that might be different. He hoped this might help trigger something, some remembrance of the dream, so that he might figure out what was happening.

By the time the lecture was finishing, he'd seen nothing untoward. Nothing that spoke to any hidden memories. He was none the wiser. In fact, he had spent the last ten minutes just watching Jennifer and Elizabeth aimlessly.

Noticing the lecture hall emptying he shrugged off the idea that another dream was coming true and grabbed his things and tried to catch up to Elizabeth and Jennifer who he could see were just exiting through the doorway.

Barely three steps into the corridor, Jonathan felt his head snap back, his legs go from underneath him, and he crumpled backwards down onto the floor. Audible gasps came from the other students who were stood around.

He was completely taken by surprise and looked up from his pronate position on the floor, trying to reconcile what had just happened. He'd struck his head on the floor and was still a little dazed, the faint smell of concussion in his nostrils. But, he could see the blurry vision of a couple of girls, one bent over him asking if he was alright the other berating someone behind them, and who were out of his vision.

He slowly made his way to his feet and could see a couple of guys who looked vaguely like some of Josh's friends walking away sniggering to themselves.

From the corner of his eye, he became cognisant of a mass of brown hair on his shoulder. He took half a step away, thinking it was one of the girls who had helped him up, but then she had silky auburn hair, not the dull wavy brown hair he'd seen.

The realisation swept over him like a leopard pouncing in slow motion and he raised his hand to the back of his head.

There it was. He could feel it.

At that moment Jennifer and Elizabeth appeared from the crowd of students. He couldn't let them see him like this, not till he had gotten his head around both what had happened, and how.

He bolted towards the nearest toilets so he could inspect himself and think in a bit more privacy.

"Jonathan!" called Jennifer, seeing him first.

"Back in a tick!" he called behind himself, hands covering the back of his head as he ran off.

The last thing he heard was the auburn-haired girl saying something to Jennifer. No doubt filling her in on what had happened.

Inside the toilets he looked at himself in the mirror, tilting his head from side to side to try see as much as he could. From what he could see there was a patch of hair, roughly the size of a small fried egg, and about twelve inches long sprouting from the back of his skull. It reminded him a little of a meat grinder, the way mince hung out of the back of the machine in long streams. He looked like someone who had put on a crash helmet backwards, his hair falling from a small area that was uncovered by what would have been the helmets face front. In short, he looked, and felt, silly.

He had not dreamed *this*, he felt sure if it. Hair, yes. A bald ponytail, no. He needed to remove it.

He had scissors and a beard trimmer at home, but he had to get there first. He stood, staring at himself in the mirror as he weighed up his options. Then it occurred to him. If this was a dream, albeit one he had very little recollection of having, would everyone already be used to him having this thing sprouting from the back of his head? Was it just him not used to it? If they were, then he was feeling silly for no reason. On the other hand, there was an equal likelihood that they were as ignorant of the fact as he was, in which case, they may look at him like he was an alien, or worse yet, they would have yet another thing with which to ridicule him mercilessly, exactly as they had when he'd first shaved his head. What was he to do? keep it covered and hope for the best, or stay as it was and try style it out?

Styling things out was not his forte, and if this was a case of a dream coming true, then he was starting to have very mixed feeling about how good the whole affair was.

He tucked his hair into his jacket collar, pulled the hood up and turned and walked out of the toilets with as much determination as he could muster.

Elizabeth and Jennifer stood outside, waiting for him.

"Are you okay?" asked Elizabeth quizzically "a girl said someone had grabbed your hair and dragged you to the floor?"

"Yes, I'm alright." Jonathan replied, continuing his brisk pace. "No harm done except a little embarrassment."

"Good. And since when did you have hair?" asked Jennifer, following on behind, and with an amused smirk on her face, as though about to make some sarcastic comment, but just managing to contain herself.

'Damn' thought Jonathan to himself. Clearly, they weren't already aware, as he had hoped.

"I don't know" he replied "Come on, let's get out of here and I'll try explain". And with that he marched off back to his apartment, leaving them to continue following if they wanted. He needed to cut it off anyway, and he wasn't bothered if they were present or not when he did. As it turned out, they kept following, repeatedly asking how long he'd had hair and whether he might let them see it.

Jonathan somehow managed to ignore them all the way back to his apartment. They were like children, and he spent the time trying to figure out if this was something he might dream; half his mind saying no, there was no way he would dream something so annoying, the other half saying yes, this was just too silly to be the rational actions of two women of their age.

As soon as he got into the apartment, he headed straight for the bathroom, leaving the door open for the two of them to follow, which they did just seconds after him.

"Okay," he said resignedly. "you want to see it, fine. You can help me cut it off. I hate it already." and with that he tipped back the hood from his head and took off the jacket.

From where they were stood, they couldn't see anything different to begin with, but when Jonathan turned his head from side to side, they could see the length of wavy brown hair moving about like a horse's tail.

The pair of them stood in shocked silence, mouths agog. When the auburn-haired girl had said Jonathan had had his hair pulled, they never imagined it would be as long as this. They had thought it was just a short tuft, maybe a few inches long. Thinking it had to have been relatively short in order for him to have kept it concealed from them, but this was about a foot long, and nothing like what they had imagined. How could it have grown to this length without them noticing?

"Oh. My!" said Elizabeth "Is it real?"

"What do you mean 'is it real', of course it's real. What else could it be?" replied Jonathan, somewhat baffled

"I thought it might have been hair extensions. Given that we hadn't noticed you had any hair, previously... You shaved it all off ages ago, remember? I didn't realise you'd left a bit at the back. I can understand you keeping it covered though. It would have looked odd, and considering the comments you got when you shaved it, I can understand you not wanting anyone to know." said Elizabeth by way of a vague explanation. "Given that we've never seen you with any hair, not since, then it's natural to think you'd only have a small patch and gotten extensions added."

Jonathan looked at her confused.

"You're telling me people cut their hair short, and then put fake hair extensions in to make it look long again? ... That makes absolutely no sense." he began, then realised he had a more pressing concern. "Never mind, come on, help me cut it off." and he reached over his shoulder, grabbed as much of the hair as he could, pulled it as high and straight as possible and cut through it with the scissors.

This should have severed around eight or nine inches of hair from the length. However, when he let go of it to drop it on the floor, it merely returned to its previous place, still fully attached.

"What the?!" he mumbled, confused. Were his eyes failing him? He looked at Elizabeth and Jennifer, and they both bore the same confused look, clearly it wasn't just him.

"You mustn't have cut it right." said Jennifer, also trying to convince herself that her eyes hadn't just deceived her. "Here, let me."

Jonathan passed her the scissors, and she grabbed as much of the hair as she could get her hands to.

"Not so hard." he said as his head was yanked back.

"Shut it you wuss." she replied, and took the scissors to the hair. The same thing happened again. When she dropped the hair, it merely fell back into place as though nothing had happened. Not so much as a single strand had been severed. Jennifer was dumbfounded. Her eyes saw the scissors cut through the hair, and yet when she let go, she also saw it all fall back exactly in place completely unharmed.

"How is that possible?" she asked quietly.

"What?" asked Jonathan over his shoulder.

"I've just cut it off...I swear I did...and it's still there ... How are you doing that?" she asked him, unbelievably confused. She felt like she was a little girl being tricked by a magician's sleight of hand, except it was her own hand doing the sleighting.

"You can't have cut it then." said Elizabeth from behind her.

"I saw the hair break from the scissors when I cut it." Jennifer snapped back at her. "Come on, let's try again."

She tried once again, with the exact same result. She stood, staring at it, aghast.

"This is freaking me out." she said, confusion now beginning to overwhelm her. "How does it do that?!"

Jonathan signed. "I think I need to tell you something." but Jennifer wasn't paying attention to him, she was still staring fixedly at the puzzle before her, determined to figure it out.

"It's impossible." she said "Elizabeth, get your phone out. I want you to film me cutting it off this time." Elizabeth took her phone from her pocket, opened the camera, swiped across to set it to video mode and held up to the back of Jonathan's head, making sure to get the best angle she possibly could.

"Okay ready." she said to Jennifer when she was in position. Jennifer once again took hold of the hair and closed the blades of the scissors, watching the strand of hair snap as the blade bit through them.

Chapter VII

Once again, when she let go to drop the length of hair to the floor, it just fell back into place as though it had never been cut.

"Oh. My. God!" exclaimed Elizabeth who had finally seen the miracle up close with her own eyes. Like Jennifer, she could not believe them. She stood staring in utter disbelief, exactly as Jennifer also was.

"I'm trying to tell you." said Jonathan, a little louder this time, making sure to get their attention.

"What?" asked Jennifer, as though that, even though she had heard him speak, she'd not heard what he'd said. He turned round to face them both.

"It's my dreams." he said. He really didn't know how this conversation was going to go, even though he knew that what he was saying, and what he knew, still felt strange, even to him, but he thought he might as well get directly to the point, and then attempt a clearer explanation later.

Both Jennifer and Elizabeth continued to stare incredulously, this time at his face instead of the back of his head.

"What *are* you talking about?" asked Jennifer, emphasizing the 'are' so it was clear to him she thought him a simpleton.

"My dreams," he repeated, still unable to think of how to explain this coherently. "they're coming to life... Last night... I dreamt I had hair ... Only, not like this. Proper hair, on my head, not this. I don't know how *this* happened... I don't remember dreaming this bit, but I dreamt I had hair and then this morning I woke up and I had! ... Although I didn't notice at first as I was late for the lecture ... But it didn't matter, because I'd already had that lecture a week ago as it happened... Before Josh beat me up... So, I already had notes on it..."

"Woah!" said Elizabeth, raising her hands "you're babbling. Go back. You're not making any sense at all...Hair? ... Dreams...Josh ... Beaten up...Who's Josh? and when did he beat you up?"

It was Jonathan's turn to stare incredulously now. How did they not remember, it hadn't been that long ago.

Then it occurred to him.

"That's right. People that are in the dreams don't seem to remember them happening." he said, mostly to himself. And then, after a few more seconds thought. "So how am I supposed to know what's a dream and what's real life?" he felt a little dejected at his conundrum, and caused him a great deal of concern.

The look of confusion Jennifer and Elizabeth were feeling was not changing, and an intense concentration was written all across Jonathan's face as well, as he stared intently into nothingness and contemplated the conundrum. They were all as equally confused as one another.

He also needed to think of how to explain things to them, given that they had no memory of events. It would have been much simpler to explain things, so they would believe him, if they too were able to at least recall any of the events.

"Okay." he said finally. "You remember a couple of weeks ago; we were getting a takeout down the high street? where we go to that coffee shop to study?" He'd have to feel his way through events in order to establish what reality was, and therefore what they could also recall, and what were his dreams, and therefore, they couldn't. He didn't for one moment think this was going to be easy, but he had no other options available to him at this time.

"Yeah." they replied in unison. Jonathan felt himself relax a little inside, at least they remembered this. It was a starting point.

"And you remember those Jocks that were making fun of me?"

"Yeah."

"Right." he felt he was now beginning to make a little progress, albeit slowly. "Well, that night I dreamt that I actually stuck up for myself, you know, had a smart answer to knock them down a peg or two. Well, that dream came true the next day. We had the lecture on social psychology where he was telling us about Freuds theory of Eros and

Thanatos. Then we went to the coffee shop to study for a while. Do you remember any of that?"

"I remember us being at the coffee shop, but I don't remember the lecture beforehand. And it can't have been the one you said as we only just had that today." replied Elizabeth. "Are you sure you're not misremembering?"

"No." replied Jonathan, honestly.

He needed to think. They remembered some events, but not others, maybe this was where real life and dream life were starting to mix.

"Do you remember what we did after the coffee shop?" he asked, probingly, hoping that she might somehow remember the right things.

"Hmm!?" she thought "I remember we were in our apartment, but you weren't there, so I guess we must have split and went home."

"So, you don't remember us bumping into the Jocks again? he asked.

"No." they replied, looking at each other, still confused.

"Oh." replied Jonathan, a little disappointed. But this was good, he seemed to have found the point where the reality and the dream were separated. "Okay. Well, I guess that means that somewhere between us leaving the coffee shop and us meeting those Jocks must be where my dream starts, and it must end when I'm back in my apartment and you guys have left." he said, again thinking to himself but saying it out loud.

"Hang on." said Jennifer, still confused, but starting to think Jonathan was now winding them up. "You're expecting us to believe that you are having little adventures that only you know about, and you expect us to believe these are dreams you had, that are coming to life? Pull the other one!"

"I'm not really expecting you to believe anything... I'm not even sure I believe any of it myself, but I know what I'm going through, and I'm just trying to figure it out myself."

"Wait." said Elizabeth suddenly. "So is this a dream. Now? Or is this real life? And how do we know?"

"No. Yes. I don't know." replied Jonathan, trying to figure out if this was still a dream or real life, himself. His mind was in overdrive trying to think it all through in any semblance of rational logic. "I dreamt I had hair, and I have hair, so that bit is dream. You guys don't remember events that happened in previous dreams, so that makes me think this is real. But when you try cut my hair, it doesn't cut, which cannot be real, so I really don't know."

"But if we don't remember events in previous dreams," said Elizabeth, very thoughtfully. "that doesn't necessarily mean this is reality, it could be a dream, right? Or do people in different dreams remember events from other dreams they have been in? Do dreams have that kind of continuity?"

Jonathan tried to think this through. "You could be right. In which case this must still be a dream coming to life, and not real reality. Or maybe it's both? and the dream life and real reality are cutting in and out of each other, intermingling, meshing into one seamless day...at least from my perspective. You guys seem to not be able to remember the bits of my dream life that you are in, so to you, you feel like either you've lost time, or you remember something else happening instead..."

"Woah!" interjected Jennifer suddenly. "You're going to need to slow down. This is giving me a headache; all this 'dream that's real for you but not real for us', and the 'reality that's real for us both but we remember something different to you if it's your dream real and not our real that's real', how are we supposed to get our head around this? Have you been hitting acid or something? this is too far out Jonathan. There's no way you can expect us to believe any of this, you know that, right?"

"I know. I'm struggling with it myself, trust me. It's happening to me, after all. I'm just trying to talk it through so I can make some kind of sense of it myself. I feel like I'm losing my mind."

"Okay," she conceded "so we're all as confused as each other. I think we can agree on that."

"Okay, agreed." Jonathan replied. He wanted to keep the conversation on track and try to figure out, between them, some semblance of a logical explanation, or at least an understanding. If they couldn't explain it, he felt reasonably sure he would never be able to explain the 'why' any of this was happening, so at least understanding 'what' was happening would be a reasonable enough consolation.

"So, we've all seen the thing with my hair, right?"

"Seen it." replied Jennifer "Believing what I've seen is another matter entirely; and it isn't making any of this the less confusing."

"No, I know." he replied "But last night I dreamt that I had hair. I'm pretty sure I dreamt I had a full head of hair, but as I woke late this morning, I didn't have time to think it over in any detail, so maybe I did actually dream I had this awful ponytail thing. But that's by-the-by. Today, I have woken up with it, one way or another, and I definitely did not have it yesterday."

"Well, we can all agree on that. You *definitely* did not have hair yesterday, which is why I thought you'd had extensions put in." Said Elizabeth, reiterating the point she'd made earlier.

"Okay." said Jonathan, sensing she was trying to cause an argument, and not wanting to waste time with pointless squabbles. "And you have tried to cut it off, as have I, unsuccessfully." he said, addressing Jennifer.

"Yes, three times. It's the damnedest thing..." she let the sentence trail off as she couldn't rationalise what her eyes had relayed to her.

"Which means," said Jonathan, picking up the conversation "that this, now, is still part of my dream." The reality dawning on him "Which means that you are not likely to remember any of this." He let himself fall into a chair, his head in his hands. It all seemed so futile. "So, I need to figure out when dream-real ends and real-real begins, and then, when we're in real-real, try to explain all this to you again."

This was a crushing blow to Jonathan, he felt he had made some headway into getting them to understand, as confusing as it was, only to realise that he'd not really explained anything to them, and that he still needed to go over this again. Which would have been okay had any of it made sense to him in the first place.

"Uhh, what?" said Jennifer, still failing to grasp most of what he was saying. "And how do we do that?" and even as these words came out of her mouth, she didn't really understand what she was asking him.

"I don't know." he replied honestly. "To me, all this seems real." and he shook his head in despair.

"Maybe we just wait it out?" said Elizabeth optimistically "It can't last forever, right?"

"Who knows?" replied Jonathan. He was still trying to work out how he'd be able to tell the different states he was in, which seemed an impossible task given everything felt as real as everything else.

"She's right." said Jennifer, who had given up, she'd decided that, in the absence of being able to formulate her own rationalisation, she would just agree with everyone and wait for something in her mind to click, at which point she would consider giving some ideas of her own. As it was, she was tired of thinking about it and wanted to get the conversation back to something she found more comfortable. More real, for her. "We might as well just carry on as normal. At some point, it will make sense, and we can talk it through then, but while none of it makes sense then let's do something we are all united in being real, and preferably, not involving talking about different realities. We've got our lecture notes, lets concentrate on that. I'm going to make some coffee and grab a paracetamol or two. This conversation has given me a splitting headache."

"Good idea." replied Elizabeth. "It's given me a thumper too; can you grab me a couple as well?"

"Yeah, no problem. Coffee?"

"Yes, thanks."

"Jonathan. Coffee?"

"Hmm? Yes, please." he said, still distracted. He wasn't thinking of anything but his current problem.

"I need to copy your notes." Elizabeth called to Jennifer in the kitchen "I was nodding off in the lecture and didn't get any decent ones."

"Okay" Jennifer called back. "They're in my bag, just grab them while I get these made and we'll start when you're done."

"I'm going to the toilet then, I'm busting." Said Jonathan, who wanted some time to think, quietly and in private.

A few minutes later he rejoined them. He still hadn't got anywhere with trying to figure anything out so had tried to put the thoughts to the back of his mind.

Jennifer had returned from the kitchen, and they were sat either side of the three-seater, waiting for him. He took a seat in the adjoining chair.

"Have you done already?" he asked Elizabeth.

"Uh?" she asked.

"Copying Jennifers notes."

"Oh." she replied, seeming a little caught out. "No, we decided I might as well just make my own as we go along."

"Okay, makes sense I suppose." he replied "Right, well he started off talking about Social confrontation, and Freuds theory of Eros and Thanatos, something about them being Greek?"

"I've heard of Eros before," said Jennifer "the god of Love. I've never heard of Thanatos though. Was he the God of hate then? if Freud is saying they are opposing powers?"

"No idea. I'll have a look." said Elizabeth. "The internet's great for that sort of info." and she took out her phone. "Oh, dammit. I've been recording. I must have knocked it when I put it in my pocket."

"No," said Jonathan, casually "you were recording Jennifer trying to cut my hair, don't you remember? you must've just forgotten to press stop."

After a moment, he became aware of the absolute silence in the room, and he raised his eyes up to look at them both. They were looking at him with expressions of blank confusion, as though he had just spoken in biblical Hebrew, or tongues.

"You have no idea what I'm talking about do you?" he asked.

They shook their heads, slowly, and in unison, the expression now switching from confusion to concern.

Jonathan suspected the switch had happened at some point in the last few minutes, but wanted to make sure, he felt the back of his head. Nothing.

"You were trying to cut my hair, but you couldn't, so you filmed it. And I was trying to explain that my dreams were starting to happen in real life, but then we realised we were still in a dream-real...Oh, never mind, it's still too confusing to go over again. How long have you been recording for?

Elizabeth checked the phone.

"About twenty minutes." she replied. "It'll have used up all my spare memory." a look of annoyance clouded her features.

"Never mind that for the moment," Jonathan replied enthusiastically, "it means we could have evidence of what we did with my hair, you cutting it and it not being cut. As well as the conversation we had afterwards where I was trying to explain about my dreams really happening, except now we are not in dream-real, we're in real-real!" Jonathan was so excited by this he almost couldn't contain himself. "Which means now you will remember."

"Why wouldn't we remember?" asked Elizabeth, stopping the phone from recording.

"For some reason, everyone in my dreams, the dream-real at least, cannot remember them when things switch back to real-real."

Elizabeth opened her mouth to ask a follow up question, realised she hadn't grasped what he had said, so closed it again and thought it through one more time. It felt a little like she was trying to comprehend the ramblings of the insane, and the attempt to do so was drawing her in as well. She screwed her eyes to try prevent it from getting in, but it was too late, she could feel the questions working their way around her brain.

"Never mind." said Jonathan, reading the pained expression she wore. "All you have to do is watch the video back and it should start to make a little more sense… Or, at least, you'll see, or re-see, with your own eyes and I won't look quite so insane."

She looked back at him a little embarrassed. Was it that obvious what she thought?

They sat together on the couch, Jonathan sat on one side, Elizabeth, phone in hand in the middle, and Jennifer on the other, and watched the playback of the recording.

They could see the side of Jonathan's head on the screen. And it clearly was Jonathan. With a ponytail emanating from the back of his skull. Elizabeth and Jennifer, sat on the couch, stared in disbelief. Jennifer could see herself now on screen, scissors in hand, cutting off a good length of hair, opening her hand to let it drop, only to see it fall back into place exactly as it had been. Still intact, not a single strand of hair appearing to have been severed.

On the couch, both Elizabeth and Jennifer did a double take, blinking rapidly as if that would help them understand what they had just seen, or thought they had seen, more. Elizabeth heard herself say 'oh, my God', on screen, exactly as she was thinking that very moment.

The image fell as Elizabeth was lowering the phone, but they could still hear Jonathan saying, 'I'm trying to tell you', and then Jennifer saying 'what?' before the screen went black. This must have been when Elizabeth had put her phone back in her pocket; but, despite losing the visual, they were still able to hear the audio, albeit slightly muffled.

They listened back on the full conversation. Everything they had said to one another, there was no denying it was them, each of them heard their own voices, yet only Jonathan could remember the conversation happening in the first place.

When the recording had finished, they all sat in silence. Elizabeth and Jennifer speechless, staring dumbfoundedly at the phone screen, Jonathan awaiting some response from them.

After a few minutes, through which neither Elizabeth, nor Jennifer, could get hold of a single thought, a single idea that might lead them to comprehension of what they had just seen. Try as they might, it was as futile as grabbing fog. Disbelief surrounded them, like a cloak. Their minds suffocating from lack of reasoning as their lungs would have from lack of air. The sensation it left behind feeling very much the same. They felt claustrophobic, panic was rising within them before the self-preservation of ignorance kicked in.

"I need to see that again." said Jennifer, disbelief beginning to be replaced by a feeling they were being tricked, as she looked towards Elizabeth for collaboration in her denial.

"Yeah. Me too." said Elizabeth, still doubtful of her eyesight. She played it back again. There was no denying it was them; they were both, categorically, hearing their own voices, and seeing themselves on screen. It definitely was Elizabeth's phone, there was no denying that either. They were at a loss. In spite of the definitive evidence before them, neither had any memory of the event occurring in the first instance.

They played it back a third time, and sat back, in silence, letting it sink in. Jonathan stood and moved back to the armchair so he could look at them both, and maybe try to answer their questions, not that he knew what was going on, or why, but at least he remembered the events first hand.

No-one spoke for several minutes, the air between them seeming thick and blocking any sound that might even consider trying to move through it.

"So... Whatever you dream about...comes true, the next day?" Jennifer said, finally. Floating the words out there, as much to herself as to anyone, as though speaking her thoughts might help her arrange them.

"It seems that way." said Jonathan.

"But the parts that are your dreams...coming true...the people involved...have no recollection of them happening...afterwards, I mean?" Jennifer continued to float out her thoughts, trying to release them slowly, so as not to implode from them.

"As far as I can tell."

They sat in silence for a little while longer, trying to process the next logical, or illogical thoughts. All they knew, was what they had seen and heard on the phone. They also knew how utterly inconceivable it all was that it should happen at all. It was going to take some time for them to get their heads around this.

"So ... You can control this?" asked Elizabeth eventually.

"Not as far as I can tell." replied Jonathan. "When I first suspected my dreams were coming to life, I spent every morning paying special attention to what I had dreamed the night before. For the first few days, I couldn't remember anything. I guess that maybe I didn't dream on those nights. Then I had this dream about having hair, although I didn't remember it...I had slept in and was late for the lecture. As I was in a rush, I didn't have time to think about it, so I didn't find out it had happened until I was in the corridor...well, you know what happened after that."

"Do we?" asked Jennifer in surprise.

"Oh, right, that was still dream-real, sorry."

"We should see if you can get anything you want." said Jennifer, a little enthusiasm creeping into her voice as she began to realise the implications. "It'll need to be specific, not like wishing for a pet or something. It'll have to be something that could only be a dream."

"I don't know," said Jonathan "Having hair hasn't exactly been a pleasure."

"We need more evidence." cut in Jennifer. "If you can dream something that you know could only be a dream, you can record it, and we can try see if we can spot anything that would help identify the things that separate the dreams from the real-life."

"And then what?" replied Jonathan "How is that going to stop anything?"

"I don't know," conceded Jennifer, "maybe it would help you control them a bit though? use them to your own advantage? it's worth a try at least, right!?"

"So, what shall I try? It needs to be something that can only be a dream, and ideally, that's harmless. I don't want to dream I'm a fighter pilot, only to crash and die."

"I don't know." she replied, and paused for a moment to think. "Man, I never thought it would be so hard to think of a dream. I can't think of anything that I dream about that I could suggest. Aside from passing my exams and driving off in a Lamborghini; but if that happened, I don't think we'd put it down as a dream, likely we'd think you were secretly the son of a millionaire and had just paid for your results instead if earning them like the rest of us."

"What about being able to fly?" asked Elizabeth, in a burst of enthusiasm "when I was a kid, I used to dream about flying all the time. That and being wonder-woman and beating up all the kids I didn't like at school." She laughed at the memory.

"Might work I guess." Jonathan shrugged "Okay, tonight I'll try dream about being able to fly. We'll see what happens."

"Let's hope we remember this conversation too." said Jennifer.

"We should," said Elizabeth, and then, suddenly doubtful "Shouldn't we? this is real-real, isn't it? not his dream-real?"

"Who knows anymore? but at least if this is his dream-real then at least we both won't remember it, so we won't be any worse off."

"What if I dream that we remember this conversation?" replied Jonathan, suddenly realising another level of complexity. "I suppose it will depend on my dream, if I even dream. If I dream that we remember, then we should remember the whole of this conversation, but how would we know if that's dream-real or real-real if my dream-real is making us think it's real-real?" Jonathan stopped; it was making his head hurt.

"That's why we need to get more evidence to see if we can spot anything that would help identify the things that separate the dreams from the real-life, otherwise we're never going to know" replied Jennifer.

Chapter VIII

He could hear music playing in the distance. A rock song, emerging from a fog. A sudden clarity as he was yanked from unconsciousness to consciousness.

He rolled over and grabbed his phone from the bedside table.

"Hello." he said, groggily.

"Well?" came the voice from the other end.

"Well, what?" he'd been awake for only ten seconds and already someone was asking cryptic questions.

"Did you dream you could fly?" the voice sounded excitable, yet familiar. His mind raced to catch up.

"Huh?" He held the phone up to his face to check the time. 08:07. "You rang me at five past eight in the morning just to ask me that? Couldn't you have waited till later?"

"No! I want to know now...well? did you?"

He thought for a moment. What had he dreamed? The phone call had distracted him, and he couldn't recollect anything. He was still very tired, yesterday had been a troublesome day and all that thinking had exhausted him.

"No" he said, and hung up.

He rolled onto his back and lay in bed, staring at the ceiling, wondering if there was any way he could control his dreams; Make sure he only dreamed what he really wanted. He thought about the dreams he'd had so far. The dream about Elizabeth, or was it Elizabeth? In his dream and in the dream-real, she had called herself Elizabeth, but she hadn't really looked like Elizabeth, and the hair colour had been different to the Elizabeth he knew, the body shape was different as well. So, if it wasn't Elizabeth, who was it?

Whatever the case, it was clearly something he had truly wanted, and it had come to life the following day. What else did he want? Consciously or subconsciously, could he even tap into his subconscious? If so, how? And how could he then try force himself to have those dreams? He thought hard and deep for a long time.

Then he had an idea.

"I can't believe you didn't dream that you could fly." said Jennifer disappointedly when they met up a little later on.

"I can't believe you phoned me at eight o'clock in the morning to ask me." he replied.

"Well. Yeah...sorry about that, but I was excited. I wanted to know. Don't you think it's amazing your dreams are coming true?"

Jonathan smiled to himself. It was the first time he could recall Jennifer being particularly excited about anything. It gave him a warmth flush inside.

"So? What did you dream then? If it wasn't that you could fly?"

"I don't really remember. It was hours ago." Jonathan replied.

"Well, you must. It's important. Think!" replied Jennifer impatiently.

Jonathan was a little affronted by the forthright nature in which Jennifer was accosting him and he didn't particularly appreciate it. But he couldn't help but agree with her, despite the way she spoke, so he gently closed his eyes and attempted to recall the contents of his nighttime theatre.

It wasn't easy, but the more he focused on what he dreamt, the more it began to come back to him. Faintly at first, but then the images began to coalesce into greater vividity.

Jennifer and Elizabeth looked on, silently and on tenterhooks for what he might divulge.

"I'm on a road…" he began.

"Walking, or driving?" Jennifer immediately interjected.

"Shh!" Jonathan replied. "I need to concentrate."

"Sorry." She whispered.

"Walking, I think? But the road seems big, somehow… a country lane maybe… hedges and trees line either side, but they all look much bigger than they should…"

"Maybe you're just small?" Jennifer interrupted once again.

"Shhh!" hissed Elizabeth.

"No, you're right. I am small. That's it... and it's as though the picture is skipping... as though I'm hopping. Like a rabbit."

"Maybe you're going to turn into a rabbit for real!" Jennifer interrupted again, almost thrilled at the prospect.

"Will you let him just tell it!" Elizabeth snapped, her patience at the constant interruptions beginning to grate on her. "We can think about that kind of thing after we've heard it all." She continued, beginning to feel a little guilty at being quite so sharp.

Jennifer held up a hand by way of apology, and made a zipping motion with the other to signify that her lips were now sealed.

"Go on." Elizabeth said, more calmly, to Jonathan.

"I hear something... something distant, and I dart off into the hedge way... then I'm by a brook or stream of some kind... but I'm in the middle of nowhere...Neither the road, nor the hedge are anywhere to be seen." Jonathan replied, staggered, as each memory came back into his mind.

Jonathan went silent for a long minute. Both Elizabeth and Jennifer held their tongues as long as their patience would allow them, but the sense of disappointment got the better of them both.

"Is that it?" asked Elizabeth. She chose to speak first as she was conscious that Jennifer had interrupted Jonathan a few times and she had shown her impatience at her for doing so. If felt like a polite way of opening things up again. A subtle climb down in the dynamic of the conversation, that also allowed her to feel as though she were apologising without actually apologising.

Jonathan held up his hand to silence her. A signal for her to give him more time to think. He still hadn't opened his eyes yet, so determined was he to focus on trying to uncover more details of the dream.

"All I can get is the vastness of the valley I am in; and all I can hear is the trickle of the water in the stream… no, wait. I follow the stream to see where it goes… I have the impression it's not the stream I'm following…I'm going towards a place where I know danger lies… I cross the stream, but the water is hitting my stomach, slowing me down… my stomach really hurts, as though I need to urinate badly, but I'm unable to go. I'm trying to force it, but it seems the harder I try the less I am able… Out of nowhere, I come across a couple of foxes who attack me… my stomach hurts really badly now… then I wake up." And at that, Jonathan opened his eyes and looked at them both, signalling that he was finished recounting the dream.

Both Jennifer and Elizabeth looked at one another for a moment or two, trying to think of what to say.

"So…" Jennifer began, but let it trail off as she realised that she had no idea what she could say next.

"So what?" Jonathan asked.

"So, what do you think it all means is going to happen to you? Are you going to turn into a rabbit? Are you going to go for a long walk in the countryside? What?"

"I have no idea." Replied Jonathan. "It's not like I have a translator in my head telling me what all this means."

"And what about you desperately needing to urinate and not being able to? What's that supposed to mean?"

"Maybe it doesn't *mean* anything?" Elizabeth postulated.

Jennifer gave her a confused look.

"We all have that dream, right? That we desperately need to urinate but are unable to. It's like our bodies know not to urinate when we're sleeping, so something deeply subconscious overrides it so that we don't."

Elizabeth could see a look of utter incredulity on Jennifers face that made her think that it wasn't quite so popular a dream as she had thought it to be.

"Come on. You're not telling me you've never had that dream?"

Jennifer remained silent.

"You're not a bed wetter, are you?"

"No, of course not."

"Well then?"

"Okay, so I guess I have had that dream." She admitted, almost disappointedly.

"Thank you! So, it's a common dream that everyone has and doesn't mean anything. It's just your every day run of the mill, innocuous dream." Then, turning to Jonathan. "What did you do when you woke up?"

"Answered the phone." He replied sarcastically, with a glance at Jennifer who screwed her face up in reply.

"After that." Elizabeth pressed.

"Went to the toilet. But everyone goes to the toilet when they first wake up, don't they. There's no way you can say it was related to the dream."

"Were you busting to go?"

"Well, yes. I guess I was."

"So, maybe, like everyone else, your dream last night was just trying to tell you that you needed to go?"

"So, what part of it is going to come true?"

“The bit about urinating!?”

“But I *didn’t* urinate in the dream, did I? that’s the point. I couldn’t. So, if that was the part that comes true, then when I woke, I wouldn’t have been able to go, would I?” replied Jonathan, following the logic of what had happened previously, and weighing it up to the current situation.

“Oh. I see what you mean.” Replied Elizabeth, suddenly understanding.

“So, what now?” asked Jennifer.

“I guess I just have to wait and see what happens.” Replied Jonathan, a little disappointed.

“So, you’ve dreamt you needed the toilet but had been unable to, and you’ve tried to dream you could fly, but that didn’t happen either. So where does that leave us?” asked Jennifer, finally.

"I don't think you *can* control your dreams though." said Elizabeth. "I tried it last night and got nothing. When we were talking yesterday it reminded me of some of the dreams I used to have as a kid. So, I tried to think of them before I went to sleep, see if I could make myself dream them again... But I got nothing ... I'd have liked to have dreamt I was wonder woman again, they were fun.” she said thoughtfully. "But I'd had hated to have woken this morning as wonder woman." She gave a little laugh at her own joke.

"It's not your dreams coming to life though, is it." said Jennifer "so you wouldn't have anyway." she turned to Jonathan, rolling her eyes.

"Well, I'm glad you think I was being serious." Elizabeth replied, cutting the conversation off.

Jonathan said nothing.

If his plan was going to work, he couldn't tell anyone. That was the only way he'd be able to find out if he could actually make himself dream about the exact thing that he had wanted to dream.

That evening, he put on a DVD and sat down to set his plan into action. It was a very specific film he wanted to watch, one that was geared specifically to what he wanted to dream that night. He thought hard about the film, as it played, and ran through the scenes imagining himself as the protagonist, adding in extra bits that he thought he would do in the same situation.

After the film had finished, he continued to think as though he were still in it, playing through new scenes and visualising how he would deal with them, how he would react. What he would do.

He kept this up whilst lying in bed, then, closing his eyes, began to utter in his head, over and over, the mantra.

"I am invisible."

Chapter IX

The same rock song woke him the next morning that had woken him for the last six months. He used to love the song, but now it just annoyed him. He changed the tune back to a more mundane ringing, and it was at that point that it struck him. He could still see his hands.

He sighed regretfully. 'Well, that doesn't seem to have worked.' he thought to himself.

Rolling out of bed, he went into the bathroom and looked at himself in the mirror. 'Yep, there I am.' He tried to think, tried to recall what he had dreamt that night. He felt sure he had dreamt. He had a vague recollection of seeing through his own eyes, but the memories seemed just beyond his grasp. He couldn't bring to mind actually doing anything in the dreams. It felt as though he had been in some kind of void all night, conscious of his being, but nothing else. No events, no actions, just emptiness. What on earth could that mean? at some point today was he going to find himself locked in a vast room with all the lights turned off? How could this be his dream? It left him puzzled. In the back of his mind, he felt another unnerving sense of foreboding.

After a quick shower, he grabbed some breakfast, and set out to meet up with Elizabeth and Jennifer. He had barely left the building when his phone buzzed in his pocket.

'We're at the coffee shop' the text read. He changed direction and made his way there, taking a shortcut past the university.

He saw the auburn-haired girl, stood with some friends, looking in his direction, so he raised a hand to wave hello. She didn't seem to notice him, so he decided against going up to her to introduce himself in case she ghosted him. He didn't like the idea of making a fool of himself again. He was an easy enough target for most people as it was. There was no need to give people ammunition.

Further on he could see Josh and his friends talking to another group of girls. These were the last people he wanted to run into, so he made a detour in order to avoid them. They seemed to be too engrossed in the girls to notice him anyway. He breathed a sigh of relief. The last thing he wanted was a repeat performance of their last encounter, or another revenge attack. He'd gotten off relatively lightly if he was being honest with himself, all things considered.

When he got to the coffee shop, he could see Elizabeth and Jennifer sat in their usual corner and he gave them a wave through the glass. They didn't appear to notice him.

He pushed the door open. There was a man sat at the table nearest the door who had his bag in the way, preventing the door opening fully and he could only get it a third of the way open. He glanced up from his coffee and newspaper, but ignored Jonathan's plight and went right back to reading his paper, leaving Jonathan to squeeze through the twelve-inch opening.

'Arsehole.' thought Jonathan, looking straight at the man as he squeezed past, and made his way over to where Jennifer and Elizabeth were sat.

"Hi." he said.

Both Elizabeth and Jennifer froze, startled, their conversation halted by a shared auditory hallucination. Their eyes scanned the room simultaneously, like a mirror image of one another.

"Did you hear that?" they asked in parallel, then looked directly into one another's face in disbelief as they realised that they had both heard the exact same thing, Jonathan saying Hi, without being able to see any evidence of him actually being present.

"I could have sworn I heard Jonathan." Elizabeth said, still looking at the spot where she thought Jonathan should have been stood.

"Me too! We must be hearing things. Maybe someone in here just sounds like him," replied Jennifer, with a half laugh, trying to rationalise what they had both heard. "He should be here soon anyway, I text him ten minutes ago, so he can't be that much longer."

"I guess you're right." Elizabeth replied, still not sure that they would both feel they heard the same thing at the exact same time. She looked around the shop, pensively, paying special attention to anyone who looked to have just arrived, but everyone she saw had already been here when they came in, or were just getting ready to leave, which made no sense as to why they might say 'hi'.

Jonathan stood staring at them both, a little unnerved by their reaction, trying to figure out if this was one of their wind-ups. He opened his mouth to speak, but in two minds as to what he should say, closed it without saying anything. He would see, if this was one of their wind-ups, just how far they were prepared to take it.

Elizabeth shivered involuntarily.

"Do you feel like we're being watched?" she asked Jennifer quietly, scanning the room once again to see what the people on the other tables were doing. They were all preoccupied with their own thing, either reading a book or newspaper, or in conversation. No one was looking in their direction, neither purposefully, nor subtly.

"Mmm, no." Jennifer replied with a slight shake of her head; but then paused as she thought about it more.

"Actually, now you mention it." and she too looked nervily around the room, imitating Elizabeth's scrutiny of the room.

Jonathan continued watching. He had to admit, their charade was convincing. The way they looked around the room was definitely done in such a way as to make him feel as if he were not there. They were doing a great job of acting as though he was invisible, managing to maintain the impression they were looking right through him. Very convincing indeed.

So convincing, in fact, that he genuinely began to wonder.

Had this been a few weeks ago, before his dreams had begun to be replicated in real life, he would have laughed this off as the girls doing one of their juvenile pranks; but it wasn't a few weeks ago, it was now. And all ideas of sensible, and sane, explanations, were out of the window and he was having to seriously consider some outlandish notions of what was now possible. So, he began to give it some serious thought.

Realising that he had not told either of them what he had planned on trying to dream, he thought to himself 'Okay, if I am, in fact, now invisible, as I had dreamed. How do I prove the theory? If I begin talking, and I am invisible, not only will they freak out in some way or another, but people at nearby table might also do so too. Okay, so I just need a non-verbal way to test this. Easy enough!'

He placed a finger of each hand into the corner of his mouth and pulled his cheeks apart. Then, he began waggling his tongue around like you might when trying to entertain an infant.

No reaction from either of them.

He stopped and studied them both carefully, looking for even the hint of a sign of a change in their demeanour. But there wasn't even so much as an inkling of a crack to the corners of their mouths that might indicate a smirk, or a smile, may be about to lighten up either of their faces.

He tried once again, this time leaning right in. To within six inches of their faces. First Jennifer, because he felt sure that, were either of them going to crack, then she would be the first. In past pranks she had always been the one to begin laughing first. He stretched his mouth, waggled his tongue, squinted and boggled his eyes, but all to no avail.

He had to stop, all that messing about with his eyes was giving him eye strain and if he wasn't careful, he'd give himself a headache.

He pinched the bridge of his nose while he thought some more.

'So, if I am invisible, how come I can see myself? It doesn't make any sense that I can see myself when no-one else can.'

He lowered his hands and looked at them, as though to reaffirm in his own mind that he could see himself. He could see them as clearly as he could see the table. He looked back at Jennifer, once again, then to Elizabeth. They had carried on with their conversation, completely ignoring him.

A rational component of his mind, that was still struggling to comprehend things, was arguing with an irrational component, that seemed to be following along just fine, over what he was experiencing.

The rational part argued that it was impossible for a human to be invisible, and, furthermore, that it could not be invisible to others whilst simultaneously being visible to himself. He was either invisible, or he was visible, and, as it was impossible to be invisible, it carried that he must be visible, therefore this was all a cruel trick being played on him by the girls.

The irrational component countered this seemingly logical argument, with the counter-argument that his dreams had now begun to be played out in real life, a thing that was also impossible, and, more so, he had already had the proof of such with his conundrum surrounding his hair, that had magically appeared, refused to be cut - several times - and then the events of him attempting to prove to the girls that his dreams were playing out in real life. How could he go to such great lengths to convince others of his unusual change of reality and still doubt it himself? It also reminded him that hair, once cut, stayed cut, and did not refuse to be cut and stay whole. This was also an impossibility. As such, the idea of 'impossible' was now obsolete and he would need to contend with the realities of the new paradigm.

The rational component of his brain was losing.

'Okay,' he thought, trying to rationalise the irrational once again 'if this is a dream, maybe I can see me because it is my dream, and even in my dream I am cognizant of my own existence, and they cannot, because they are merely characters in my dream, so they can only be, or do, what I dream they can, and they cannot be cognizant whilst within someone else's dream. In the same way that I can remember the dreams and events within them even when they are playing out again in real life, and they cannot?'

He figured this now made about as much sense as he felt it was ever likely to make to him, and decided that this was probably a good time to desist from his contemplations of it before his brain jumped out of the top of his head and made way to the nearest seaport to sail off into the sunset.

He now needed to decide what to do next. He watched the two of them continue their conversation about who they thought might be watching them; Elizabeth was still looking around the coffee shop, with suspicious eyes, searching for likely suspects.

Quick as a flash, Jonathan flicked out his hand towards her face, missing her by barely an inch.

She didn't flinch, didn't blink, not one iota of a reaction. The rational side of him needed one final piece of evidence, and now it had it. There was no way anyone could control their reflexes to that extent, especially Elizabeth, who blinked and flapped her arms around if a butterfly got within three feet of her; never mind someone's fingers flashing to within an inch of her nose. She would also have had a thing or two to say to him about nearly back handing her in the face. There was no way she would let that slide, no matter what kind of ruse she was attempting.

'Interesting.' he thought, and sighed as he finally conceded the fact that he was in fact, invisible.

They both looked in his direction again.

"You heard that? right?" said Elizabeth.

"Yeah," replied Jennifer "sounded like someone sighing, but it sounded way too close to be any one of them." and she nodded towards the others in the shop. Suddenly, she swept her hand out. Jonathan just about managed to move out of the way. Another half an inch and she would have hit him in his groin.

"Come on, this place is giving me the heebie-jeebies. Let's go." she said "I'll text Jonathan to meet us at the library instead."

Jonathan moved out of their way as they got up and he followed them out of the shop. He saw the man near the door lean down to move his bag out of the way, so Jonathan gave the door an extra push, out of Elizabeth's hand, knocking it into the man's table, spilling his coffee. He mumbled some derogatory remarks under his breath as he went to mop up the spilled beverage, so Jonathan kicked his foot out and hit the man in the side of the kneecap with his toe end, leaving him thinking he had banged it on the table leg and wincing in pain as Jonathan darted out of the door behind the girls.

Elizabeth and Jennifer were already dashing up the street. They seemed to want to get away from the coffee shop as fast as they possibly could, and Jonathan struggled to catch up.

He followed on behind them for a few minutes before deciding to give them some space. They were obviously unnerved, and he needed to think about what this all now meant for him. Not least how he could either announce his invisible self or wait until it had worn off and he was back to real-life time so he could try to explain that it had been successful after all.

He had, however, no idea how long this *would* last, so, decided he should make the best of it and eek out as much fun as he could.

Across the forecourt he could see Josh and his friends still talking to the group of girls, and he knew exactly where he would start.

He made a beeline straight for them. No-one in the group even so much as hinted at a glance in his direction as he approached, which built his confidence all the more.

He was now stood about three feet from them. He could hear Josh trying to smooth talk one of the girls, a sly, self-confident grin on his face. She, in turn acting coy and embarrassed, running her fingers through her hair. A clear signal she was reciprocating and obviously relishing the attention that she was receiving.

Jonathan stood, his gaze moving from one to the other. Neither gave any sign they knew he was there, and, while he was confident that Josh, at least, would object to his presence, he wanted to make sure. He opted for the same manoeuvre he had used on Elizabeth, and quickly flicked his hand towards Josh's face, his hand went to within a fraction of an inch of his nose, yet nothing, no reflex reaction whatsoever.

'Okay,' thought Jonathan, 'let's see how smooth you are in a minute.' and he reached forward and gently stroked the crotch of Josh's baggies for a few seconds. He managed to move his hand away when Josh gave a subconscious scratch of what, to him, felt like a light itch.

When he had stopped, Jonathan reached forward and repeated the process. He saw the self-confident grin slip from Josh's face as he felt what was happening.

Jonathan then turned his attention to the girl, gently touching her stomach, light enough for her to feel, but not so heavy that it felt like a prod. It had the desired effect, she brushed her stomach and looked down to see what it was, finding herself looking at a semi aroused Josh's crotch.

"Ergh!" she screamed and slapped him round the face. "You dirty pervert!" She grabbed her bag in front of herself as a barrier and stormed off as fast as she could calling behind her, to her friends "Come on. He's got a hard on."

At which point, her friends looked for themselves and burst out giggling and pointing at Josh, who was already flushed red with embarrassment.

Jonathan had to run away too, for fear of laughing out loud and thereby giving himself away. He inadvertently ran in the direction of the auburn-haired girl and her friends.

Something made him stop as he got closer to her. It struck him as odd that, although he had seen her a few times now, he never seemed to see her face. Now was no exception. Her hair was draped across the side of her head, obscuring her profile, just the tip of her nose peeking out from the glossy drapery of hair. He felt captivated. Something inexplicable drawing his attention. He regarded her with curiosity. What was it?

Then it occurred to him.

With the exception of the hair colour, she could have been Jennifer's twin. Same height, same build, same mannerisms. He had an unaccountable feeling of Deja-vu. He knew her somehow.

It took him a moment for it to click, but when Elizabeth had visited him in his apartment, he recalled there were differences between the Elizabeth he knew and the Elizabeth that was in the apartment at the time. He also recalled that he couldn't see that Elizabeths face either. At the time he had put that down to her state of undress and that he hadn't particularly been focusing on her face, but now he made a concerted effort to recall the moment back and remember as much detail as he could.

He still couldn't recall any discernible features of her face, and he had only accepted it was Elizabeth due to that being the name proffered to him through the door.

His head was spinning again as he tried to fit together what this all meant.

Another factor that occurred to him now, was that the Elizabeth that had appeared at his apartment, looked uncannily like this auburn-haired girl. The way she moved, her figure, her flow, all gave him sharp flashbacks to that evening in his apartment. The only difference seemed to be the colour of her hair, other than that he could have sworn it was the same person. He had so many thoughts flowing around his head now that it made him dizzy.

Was it really the auburn-haired girl that had visited him? and if so, why? He had only met her in the corridor the week after when he had been dragged to the floor by his hair. Or had he? Was that merely the first time he had, in truth, noticed her? Had he seen her before? not paid her any attention? But his subconscious clearly had. Why?

The more he looked at her, the more questions spilled into his mind, making his head swim. He felt nauseous, he needed to get away. He was feeling suffocated by all these questions, the conundrums. He needed to find the answers. He felt he was on the brink of a realisation; one that, right now, was just beyond his grasp, but he hoped would explain many of these questions, and maybe explain what was happening to him, and why. What he really needed, was to stop the bombardment of questions that span around his head. He needed to organise his thinking.

He needed a distraction.

He turned away from her, hoping that would help, and tried to fix his eyes on something else, anything else. But nothing seemed to take hold, so he set off walking. Trying to force his thoughts down a different path. He would get back to trying to have some fun with his invisibility, use his state to his advantage.

He wandered, somewhat aimlessly, around the University campus, listening to people's conversations hoping to garner some gossip about his fellow students. Sadly, this proved to be a futile, and to Jonathan, tremendously tedious endeavour. There seemed to be only three real topics of conversation, television programs, either to watch, or being watched, weekend exploits, again, either past or future plans, or subjects being studied.

The only benefit he could ascertain from all this was that it made him realise that they were all not so far different from him, contrary to past comments some of them had made to him.

It was while listening to a group of girls in conversation that he struck upon a mischievous idea. He knew it was pathetic, childish even, but it was also most teenage boys' fantasy. He would sneak into the girls' toilets to see what they got up to in there, and if indeed they did get up to the kind of things teenage boys imagined them doing. 'What good is invisibility if you cannot explore the forbidden?' the thought to himself.

He spent less than two minutes in there.

They merely had the same inane conversations, albeit with less social awareness, applied make-up and went to the toilet. Something he definitely regretted experiencing.

That particular bubble burst, he derided himself for thinking he would find some hidden mystery revealed to him. This derision then made way for disappointment which led onto embarrassment and utter shame.

Of all the times he had been bullied, been called names, none of them made him feel quite so ashamed as he now felt about his recent actions.

It was while distracted by this self-loathing that he walked, head-first into someone who knocked him flat on his back. He looked up to see a stunned, and angry Josh, looking bigger and taller than ever, staring down at him.

"Watch where you're walking arsehole!" Josh yelled and carried on walking past.

Jonathan was frozen with fear. Had he become visible again? had the girls in the toilets seen him at all? There had been no reactions if any of them had.

He looked up and down the corridor. No one else appeared to be paying him the least attention, but he still felt embarrassed - this time from walking into someone and being knocked to the ground - so he quickly scrambled back to his feet and made haste to get away.

After quickly making his way back out of the University building, he found a short wall to sit on to catch his breath and think.

Had he now become visible again? He had always been able to see himself, but had it worn off so quickly without him being aware? He needed to determine properly whether or not he was visible again. Josh had looked straight at him when he shouted, but not stopped to do anything else, and no-one else in the corridor had paid the slightest bit of attention to him, so far as he could tell. This was not something that usually happened when someone is knocked to the ground. Invariably, a few people looked, even if just to assess the situation to see if it was just someone falling over or if it was a fight about to start, which still occasionally happened.

Before he did anything else, he needed to know if he could now be seen by everyone. He reasoned that the easiest way to establish that fact, was to ask someone.

He didn't feel that walking up to someone and saying, "Can you see me?" was necessarily the best option. In all likelihood, if they could now see him, it would elicit enquiries into the stability of his mental faculties, and if they couldn't see him, would likely frighten them half to death, as a bodyless voice appearing from nowhere was a thing of quite some alarm. No, he needed a more subtle way to establish the fact.

He looked around him, a simple wave to a friend would suffice, nothing too out of the ordinary for a friend to wave at another friend, certainly not something that would make them feel he was being odd. His eyes fell on Billy, who lived in the same apartment block as he did. And he was walking towards him down the path. Perfect!

He waited till Billy was about ten yards and gave him a friendly wave.

Billy made no reaction he didn't even change his eyeline. Jonathan thought for a second. Surely, if someone waves at you, your natural instinct would be to look at them, whether you know them or not. It's almost unavoidable. So, if Billy was ignoring him for any reason - and Jonathan knew of no such reason, and Billy was not the type to not acknowledge someone - then Billy would have looked, even if he was consciously ignoring him. But Billy did not do this, Billy made no such movement. In which case, Jonathan was inclined to suspect that he was still invisible. But still, he wanted something a little more concrete.

"Billy." he called out.

Chapter X

Billy turned around at the sound of his name. It sounded close by but, when he looked, the nearest person was perhaps thirty yards away, and they had their back to him, so there was no way it could have been as loud as it appeared. He looked around further.

No-one.

Could it be that he had imagined it? Maybe he had. But he felt quite certain that someone had said his name.

"What?" he called out tentatively.

No reply.

Was he hearing things or was someone playing tricks on him? He walked over to the wall and peered over; in case someone was lying down the other side. There was no-one there.

Someone would have to be rather stupid to be lying in the snow in late January, just to play a trick on him, he thought. But where had the sound come from?

"I'm hearing things." he said quietly to himself, gently shaking his head and laughing it off.

This gave Jonathan just the confirmation he needed, and he felt a weight of stress alleviated from off his shoulders. When Billy had walked over to the wall where he was sat, it would have been impossible for him to go unseen. Even if Billy was part of some collusion to make him think he was invisible, his eyes wouldn't have lied. Billy would be unable to avoid looking at him, even for a brief instance, had he been able to see him. But when he'd said 'what?', and when he had looked over the wall, expecting someone to be there, he hadn't even hinted at looking at him. Jonathan knew then that he was still invisible.

Which did beg the question as to how Josh had been able to see him? Billy had been stood within arm's reach when he was at the wall, a similar distance. He watched Billy walk away still telling himself he was hearing things, whilst he considered what his next options were.

He was certain now of his condition, and he resolved to make the best use of it he could while it still lasted.

* * * *

Professor Malim sat in his office in quiet contemplation. He had a stack of essays on his desk. His students' latest submissions. He had finished assessing them the night before and he was taking a moment to reconsider them. Sitting back in his chair he considered the performance of the class as a whole. Overall, he was quietly encouraged by the papers the students had handed in. Most of the class showed a level of understanding of the subject matter, which was the encouraging part. A few were woefully inadequate, but there were always one or two in each class; and, as long as it stayed at just one or two, he was confident he'd be able to bring them up to standard with some personal tuition, or even just a little guidance to get them back on the right track.

However, much to his surprise, a couple of students showed an extraordinary level of understanding, one of them even making points he himself had not considered. It was every tutor's ideal to have a student of such talent. He gave a faint smile to himself; this would reflect well on him.

Then, he unexpectantly shuddered. The hairs on the back of his neck standing on end, as though someone had just walked over his grave.

He looked up from the papers and scanned the room. He had the strangest notion he was being observed. He got up and crossed over to the door and opened it. It had been firmly closed but he looked out onto the corridor anyway, it was empty. He still had the unnerving sensation someone was watching him. He turned towards the window, a ludicrous notion as he was two floors up and the idea that someone could scale the outside wall was as ridiculous as the idea of him being able to feel someone walking across his future grave. He gave his head a gentle shake, as though to throw off the sensation, this wasn't an Edgar Allen Poe tale, after all, and he sat back into his chair, still gazing around the room for anything that seemed amiss and listened intently.

All he could hear was the rush of air through his nose from his own breathing. He gave his head another shake, but he still could not get the idea of being watched from out of his mind. He got up and walked over to the coffee percolator on the side desk.

He'd bought the percolator a few years ago after getting tired of complaining about the cheap, bitter, watery coffee that was being served at the canteen. He'd come to the conclusion that there was no need to complain about something he had it within his power to do something about, so he'd simply bought his own and since then had been able to enjoy coffee just how he liked it, and whenever he wished. Not, however, just now, as it was empty.

As he had no water supply in the office it meant he needed to go down to the bathroom to fill it from the sink. Not ideal, but hardly too great an inconvenience. His door was left ajar as he made his way down to the sink to fill the jug.

When he returned to his office a few minutes later, the first thing he noticed was that the door seemed to be more ajar than it ought to have been. He'd pulled it closed too behind him; he knew it wouldn't close entirely as the latch was too firm, but it didn't seem likely that it would have pinged back this far. He tentatively pushed the door all the way open and scanned what he could see of the room.

Was it possible someone had arrived while he was in the bathroom and was waiting?

The office was empty. He frowned, something felt very suspicious. Although the office was empty, someone must have been here. There had to have been for the door to be so far open; he had only been down the corridor, if someone had wanted him, surely, they would have come down and knocked on the bathroom door, or even just called out for him. It occurred to him, as well, that he should have heard footsteps. The corridor wasn't carpeted, and he usually could. Unless someone was barefoot? but why would someone want to see him and be barefoot. He wasn't thinking logically.

He went into the office and had a look around for any sign of theft, it was the only other reasonable explanation he could think of.

He stopped, poured the jug of water into the percolator and set it in place ready to collect the coffee as it filtered through.

He chastised himself. He was being silly, overthinking the situation and making it to be more than it was. The simple solution was that he had left the door more open than he had thought and his mind had, combined this with the sensation of being watched, turned it into some kind of film noir style malevolence. He watched the coffee percolate while he berated himself for being so illogical. He was Psychology professor after all and should be above such misrepresentation of the facts.

Coffee made, he sat back into his chair and set to the task of his reason for being in the office in the first place. That was not to allow his ego to wax lyrical on how successful some of his students were, nor was it to manifest mysterious occurrences, it was to go through the notes for this week's lecture and make sure everything was in order. He bent to retrieve the notes from his satchel and noticed the buckles of the satchel were unfastened. He regarded them with curiosity for a second before opening the bag up.

There was, unquestionably, something different about the contents of the bag. A moments inspection revealed his lecture notes were not there.

He hadn't been imagining anything after all, someone had been in his office and stolen his notes. Given that the rest of his office was undisturbed, it could only have been one of the students. But which one?

* * * *

The hardest part of getting hold of the lecture notes hadn't been getting into Professor Malim's office - all he'd had to do was follow him in - he'd just walked right in behind him making sure to duck out of the way when he closed the door behind him; all this involved was a bit of quick footwork, and timing.

It wasn't even getting the papers out of his satchel, they were simple buckles that held the leather flaps down, no locks to negotiate. Nor was it getting out of the room. At worst he thought he'd have to wait around for a while until the Professor had finished and went off to the next class he was teaching, it had been fortuitous that he had left to get more water for the coffee percolator.

No, the difficulty lay in transporting the papers from the office back to his apartment. The first part of the journey was simple, he just needed to get out of the room and off down the corridor. Easy with an empty corridor, it wasn't until he was halfway down the staircase that his paranoia revealed itself. Whilst he was invisible, were the papers? If they were not then anybody he encountered, whilst not able to see him, would be able to see a file full of papers apparently floating off on an undetermined journey. Any sensible, or mildly inquisitive person would, naturally, be alarmed at such a sight and either raise a cry of alarm, or follow said floating item to its final destination; natural intrigue of the unusual on the individuals part dictated as much.

As such, Jonathan had to behave as though they were, and navigate a route back to his apartment that took him very much 'around the houses' so as to avoid encountering anyone. Indeed, on the journey back he had to make several stops whenever he encountered someone he could not widely avoid. On one occasion diving over a wall, with all the grace of some kind of giant invisible cat, into a drift of snow; and another shoving his hand behind a foul-smelling dumpster which resulted in him getting a particularly vile smelling slime stuck to the back of his hand making him retch several times.

He finally managed to navigate his way back to the apartment unnoticed and spent the first ten minutes washing his hands repeatedly. He didn't want to know what the slime was, nor where it originated, but he absolutely wanted all traces of it off his skin.

Once the vile stench from his hand had been replaced by the fragrant perfume of soap, he made himself a coffee and sat down to read through the notes he had just obtained. His invisibility had, so far, lasted almost the whole day and, on reflection, had not been all he expected it to be.

* * * *

He woke up feeling more tired than he had been when he went to sleep the previous night. He had studied the notes into the early hours of the morning, writing up his own notes and cross referencing them, but his fatigue was not the worst of his problems. It occurred to him that he had two issues he needed to resolve as an immediate priority. The first being that he had to return the notes back to the professor; this led him to his second problem - he had to establish if he was still invisible or not.

He opted to tackle the second problem first, as it seemed evident that the solution to the first was dependant, heavily, on the solution to the second.

It was while staring in the mirror, pondering this very question, that an idea occurred to him, and he could have kicked himself for not considering this yesterday, as it wouldn't have had to run the proverbial gauntlet to get the papers back to his apartment if he had.

His idea ran thus: his problem lay, mainly, in the fact that other people were unable to see him, but that he could see himself, his hair, skin and even his clothes - and herein lay the kicker - if people could not see him, as he was, then his dream induced state of invisibility must extend to his clothing too. Otherwise, they would see him via the moving clothes, and this they had not! - more than likely, he presumed, because he very rarely dreamed of being naked - in which case he could have transported the file by simply pushing it under his jacket.

He was interrupted in his musings by a knock at the door. Startled, he did just that, shoved the file up his sweater.

"Jonathan? are you in?" came a voice. "We haven't seen you for two days. Are you alright?"

It seemed the solution to both of his problems had just presented itself. All he had to do was answer the door. If they could see him, he was no longer invisible, if they couldn't, then he knew what his next steps were going to be.

He opened the door.

It was Jennifer, who's eyes dropped, and face opened up in a look of alarm. Jonathan looked down too, doubting for a split second that he had put trousers on, but he saw straight away that he had.

"What's up?" he asked. Jennifer gave out a yelp of surprise.

"Jonathan? Where are you?" she said, peering into the apartment "and why is there a folder hovering in your doorway?"

"Damn!" he said, dejectedly. "You'd best come in."

"Err. Okay" she said cautiously "but where are you?"

"Right in front of you." he replied, which was, to him, a statement of the obvious. She took a half step backwards. His voice sounded to be coming from the folder, which she saw move in a sweeping ninety-degree arc, to one side. It quickly occurred to her that this might be another one of his dreams and that, somehow, he had dreamed he was a folder, which sounded to her rather odd even as she thought it. But then, people have the strangest dreams so it couldn't be beyond the realm of possibility.

"Have you dreamt you're a folder?" she asked tentatively. The sensation it gave her, that someone could dream their way to being a folder, not less her actually conversing with it, made her feel as though she herself was dreaming, or having some strange hallucinogenic episode that made her doubt each and every one of her faculties.

"Eh? No," replied Jonathan "I dreamt I was invisible. Here let me take this out from under my sweater."

"Wait, no don't!" she replied quickly. "If that's where you are then I think I'd prefer you to keep it there. At least I know where you are then."

"Good point." Jonathan agreed. Jennifer walked in, manoeuvring, in a comically overexaggerated way, past the folder.

"So...?" Jennifer asked.

"So, it seems I may have got that bit wrong." he said, answering his own question, not Jennifers.

"What bit?" she asked, confused.

"Uh? ... Well, I'm invisible...my skin, hair, nails et cetera, as well as my clothes. I thought that if I put the folder up my sweater that that would also become invisible too, but, as you can see it, that seems not to be the case. I'm wondering if it's only the things I have dreamt about being invisible that are, and, as I must clearly wear clothes in my dreams, then they are invisible, but not any object that's not on me."

Jennifer was momentarily baffled at this.

"But how does your dream know what clothes to make invisible?" which seemed the obvious question for her to ask.

"I've not figured that out yet." he replied, then turned and walked towards his bedroom. "Can you come in here?" he called back to her "I want to do an experiment."

Jennifer followed him in, or, more precisely, she followed a folder as it floated into the bedroom.

A drawer opened, seemingly of its own accord.

"Can you see the clothes in this drawer?" he asked. She took a step closer and peered in.

"Yes." she replied, and then watched a pair of socks levitate.

"What about now?" he followed up.

"Yep. Still see 'em. Floating there in mid-air like that's an everyday thing."

"Interesting." He said, and dropped the socks onto the bed before sitting down.

Jennifer saw the socks lay themselves down on the bed and then the cardboard folder floated down a little and tilted forwards at the same time as a curved indentation appeared on the bed.

"You're sat down." she said. She wasn't sure why she felt the need to tell him. He obviously knew that he had just sat down, but it seemed natural that she inform him that she also knew.

"You can see me?" he asked, thinking maybe it had finally worn off.

"No. I just saw the bed move ... and the folder, of course."

"Oh."

Jennifer then saw a shoe appear from out of nowhere, a surreal experience, as though a Salvador Dali painting was happening in real time. One of the socks floated from the bed, where it had previously lain, to the floor next to the shoe, another sock appeared, again, from thin air, and then both the first sock and the shoe disappeared. She stared at the event, mesmerised. She didn't hear Jonathan, at first, when he asked her.

"Can you see the sock now?" and he had to repeat himself.

"I can see *a* sock now. I can also see a random shoe that has just appeared." she said, unable to believe what she was saying, never mind what she was seeing. "I've seen a sock float from the bed to the floor, a shoe and sock appear, like magic, from thin air, then the sock disappear and I'm talking to a cardboard folder that's floating a few inches off a bed. I think I'm about five seconds away from the looney bin."

"Yeah, sorry. I guess it is a bit much isn't it? I'm not really dealing with it too well myself. But I need to try figure one or two things out." he said by way of reassuring her. "I should probably go through it with you from the beginning. Come on, let's go back to in the room and I'll try explain."

They returned to the living room and sat, whilst Jonathan attempted to take her through the events of the last couple of days.

"So, you've been like this for a full day?"

"Yes, just over."

"How long does it last?"

"I don't know. All the other dreams have only lasted an hour or two at most."

"So, how do you become visible again?" Jennifer asked after a short pause. This was all a bit much. With his previous story about dreaming he had hair, she had thought it something of a stretch, and she was inclined to believe he had been playing some kind of trick on them. It seemed more likely to her that he had grown a short stump of hair, managing to conceal it from everyone, and then having extensions applied. They had gone along with it as it was harmless, although a dumb trick to try pull, still harmless. The trick of them cutting his hair, but it not actually cutting, that baffled her to such an extent that she had opted to simply forget it had ever happened even though she had seen it played back from the recording. But now this! This was beyond 'too much'; it was blowing her mind. There was no way he could fabricate this. Even while she'd been talking to him, she had been looking for thin wires that things could be attached to, but there was nothing. His voice sounded like he was only sat a few feet in front of her as well. There was absolutely no way he could rig all this up. Not even Penn and Teller could explain this! So, it had to be true. In spite of every sane, logical, part of her brain screaming that 'this cannot be true!'.

"I honestly don't know." he replied, sounding dejected. "I'm still hoping it'll wear off. It's not all it's cracked up to be, isn't this."

They sat together and thought for a while. Jennifer could empathise with Jonathan. Even though she had never been invisible herself, no-one had, she could imagine that, whilst most would think that being invisible and having a near endless amount of fun with it would be truly spiffing, very few would consider the problems it might also carry.

"Well," she said eventually "you said that to become invisible you watched the movie, then told yourself, repeatedly, that you were invisible, before going to bed, dreaming, and then you woke up like this. What if, tonight, you do the same thing, except in reverse, and try dream that you're visible?"

"I don't think there's any movies about invisible people becoming visible though." he replied, trying, and failing, to avoid sounding sarcastic.

"Well obviously not that bit, dumbass, but the talking-to-yourself-self-hypnosis bit?"

"Yeah, sorry," he felt a bit out of order being so sarcastic, she was only trying to help. "I was thinking the same thing myself. Great minds, eh?" he gave her an apologetic smile, but then realised she couldn't see him, so it was pointless. "What am I supposed to do until tonight though? and what if I'm still like this tomorrow? I'll need to buy food at some point. How am I supposed to do that? people will freak out if they see food floating down the supermarket aisles."

Some of the more problematic aspects of invisibility were now beginning to present themselves to him.

"Well, Elizabeth and I can do some shopping for you." replied Jennifer.

"And what if this is permanent?" Jonathan interrupted "you can't do my shopping forever. And what about Uni? How am I supposed to attend lectures? and sit exams?"

"Hmm..." said Jennifer, thoughtfully. She needed to choose her words carefully, she could tell from his tone of voice that he was starting to get a tad irate, but there was no other way to say it other than directly. "Well, I guess you're going to have to try harder tonight, aren't you?"

Jonathan was glad to be invisible right now, as he knew his face would have spoken a thousand words, but he couldn't contain himself.

"Try harder! is that all you've got? I need to 'try harder'! what kind of help is that?" he knew that he was shouting, but he didn't care.

"What else is there?" she shouted back, matching his frustration.

He stared at her a moment as the dejection began to set in. She was right, he was powerless against this, and that was the only thing he had right now. They sat for a few minutes allowing themselves some time to calm down. They both knew that shouting at each other was of no help.

"I'm going to go get Elizabeth, fill her in on what's happened and see if she has any ideas." she got up and left him to fret by himself "we'll get you some shopping in whilst I'm out." she finished off with; her way of extending an olive branch.

She needed some time to herself too, to go through what she had seen in the last hour or so, and think about the latest turn of events, in what was the peculiar spectacle, that was Jonathan's life.

Chapter XI

Jennifer, basket in hand, wandered around the supermarket, trying to decide what groceries to get for Jonathan. She wished now that she had either made a list, or at least gotten some idea from Jonathan as to what he needed.

She knew she could text him, or ring him in seconds, but she was still sore from the argument they had just had, and her stubbornness prevented her from doing the sensible thing. Plus, she also wanted some time to let her emotions dissipate, so he would have to make do with whatever she bought him.

Wandering up and down the aisles, it occurred to her how dichotomic the complete normality of it was, when she compared it to the bizarrities she had been witness to with Jonathan.

Everyday people browsing the items on the shelves, making mundane choices over which brand to opt for? Countless mindless trivialities that constituted a normal day, in the normal life, of normal people. People who aren't invisible, whose hair doesn't refuse to be sheared and for whom are blissfully ignorant of anything outside the narrow sphere of their own existence.

It was such a grounding experience that it made her smile. More than that, it made her want to escape from all the insanities that she was currently wrapped up in and be a part of everyday normality.

She embraced the opportunity that presented itself and spent the next twenty minutes thinking of nothing more than which loaf of bread to get? which brand of beans? which microwave meals to buy? And whether or not should she get some of those little bio-yoghurts. She'd heard somewhere that they were good for digestion, and they had some benefits to brain function as well, but she couldn't remember exactly how.

All the anger of the argument with Jonathan, and those little stresses of trying to help him solve each problem as they arose, lifted from her shoulders, like rainwater evaporating in a middays sun. The Tao of shopping.

The queue at the checkout was four people deep, so she used the waiting time to call Elizabeth.

"Hey Liz."

"Oh, hiya Jennifer, what's up?"

"Are you doing anything right now?"

"Not really. The T.V is on, but I'm not really watching it."

"Can you come meet me at the supermarket?"

"I guess so. What are you doing at the supermarket? We only did our shop the other day."

"I'm picking up a few things for Jonathan," then, realising she was surrounded by strangers, who, although not purposefully eavesdropping, would, nevertheless, listen in, so she could hardly say 'while he's invisible' as though that were a normal thing to say in the middle of the supermarket, she opted for "while he's bedridden."

"Jonathan's bedridden? Is he sick? what's up with him?"

"I can't really talk at the moment. Come meet me at the supermarket and I can explain everything to you."

"I'll be right there. What's the weather doing?"

"Look out of the window. Just get here as quickly as you can." replied Jennifer, hanging up.

The apartment door opened of its own accord, or so it seemed to Elizabeth and Jennifer shortly after they knocked.

"Where are you? asked Elizabeth cautiously. Jennifer had brought her up to date on the latest situation whilst they walked from the supermarket.

"Right here." came the reply.

"Where's the folder?" asked Jennifer.

"I took it out. I can't walk around everywhere with a folder shoved up my sweater. It gets annoying after a while."

"Yeah, I could imagine. We'll have to think up of some alternative way of being able to see where you are until this wears off."

"If it wears off." replied Jonathan, sulkily.

"Now, wherever you are, move out of the way so we can come in and get these into the cupboards." she said, holding up the bags of groceries they had bought for him.

"I am out of the way." he replied, after stepping to one side.

Jennifer emerged from the kitchen, after putting Jonathan's groceries into the cupboards, with a piece of paper in her hand. Along one edge of it was a strip of Sellotape.

"Here, stick this on your chest" she said, passing it to Jonathan. He took it from her and read the front. 'I'm here' it said, with a thick black arrow pointing upwards. He stuck it to his chest as instructed.

"Effective." he said sardonically.

"You betcha!" replied Jennifer, equally sardonic. "But at least we know where you are now. And where your face is! This isn't our fault you know."

Jonathan understood the veiled threat within her comment, and he decided to quit while he still could.

"Good idea." he replied, more seriously, and he pressed the tape to his chest in an overly histrionic display to emphasise the point.

"So, what will you do if this ends up permanent?" Elizabeth asked, breaking up the mild tension that was building.

"Honestly, I don't know," replied Jonathan "but if I do eventually get back to normal, I'm going to be very careful about what I dream in future."

"Do you think that's possible?" asked Jennifer.

"What do you mean?"

"Can you be careful about what you dream? Don't they happen subconsciously? How will you be able to be careful not to dream something?"

Jonathan was silent for several long seconds as he considered the point.

She was right, with the exception of this last dream, he hadn't had any control over what he had dreamt, and, until he figured out how he had actually done this, and more to the point, how to undo it, he had nothing to indicate that he could actually control his dreams at all. After all, this could have just been an outrageous coincidence.

"I have absolutely no idea." he replied honestly. "It was only a couple of weeks ago that my dreams started to happen in real life, as far as I know; and it was only yesterday that I tried, of my own volition, to dream something quite specific. Even that may have just been coincidence. At this point in time, I have no idea what is possible. I do know one thing for certain though." he said, adamantly.

"What's that?" asked Elizabeth.

"I'm going to think very carefully about what I decide to dream about in future, especially if I try to dream something specific; and I'm definitely going to think of both the best and the worst possible outcomes."

"And what about the ones you don't try?" asked Jennifer, more practically. "The random ones that you don't even think about? the ones you have no control over? What about those?"

He thought the matter through for a while.

"Well, on the plus side, those ones only seem to last an hour or so at most, so I can probably cope with them, as long as they're not too out there." he said appearing more ambivalent to the problem than he really was; something he rectified as soon as he saw the look on Jennifer's face - which warned him not to be so flippant.

"But you're right. Until I get this fully figured out, I need to try find a way to have dreamless nights." he replied. After a minute he noticed Elizabeth staring at him.

"What?" he asked.

"Well. You just admitted how hard it is control what you dream about, and now you think you're going to control *if* you dream as well? as though you have any control over that either!"

This was a dose of reality he really wasn't prepared to consider at this point in time. The whole thing was too bizarre, surreal even, and he couldn't help but feel that the surrealness wasn't helping. It made him doubt whether any of this was even happening at all.

* * *

When Jonathan went to bed that night, he spent almost half an hour in the bathroom, staring at himself in the mirror, telling himself he *was* visible, in the same mantric fashion as he had previously, concentrating on not just saying the words, but believing them too. The importance of tonight played heavily on his mind and it was worrying him to distraction, which made it even more difficult to commit himself to his current task. No matter how many times he told himself, there was that voice in his head saying, 'what if'.

When he finally came to lie down, he found himself completely unable to sleep. After tossing and turning for over an hour, he decided he needed to get out of the apartment. He was comforted by the fact that, as it was nighttime, there were a considerable number of people fewer out and about. The notion came to him that he might go for a run.

He wasn't, by any stretch of the imagination, a fitness enthusiast, and he wasn't prone to running ordinarily, in fact, it had been several years since he last did, likely a PE class in school, he thought, disregarding the times he had run from bullies, but he had a lot of nervous energy pent up and he needed to burn some of it off.

He set off slowly, and gradually built up his pace until he had reached an all-out, for him, run. He then ran as fast, and for as long as his lungs and legs would sustain him. By the time his burning lungs and jellified legs had brought him to an exhausted stop, he had been running almost five minutes. Thankfully he had had the foresight to do laps of the grounds of his apartment building, so he had ended up only a few dozen yards away from the entrance way. But this took him a further five minutes due to his state of utter exhaustion, coupled with the necessity to hide his heavy guttural breathing from the one unfortunate soul who happened to be returning home from somewhere in the early hours of the morning.

After a hot shower he crawled back into bed, legs still throbbing from the exertion, and fell asleep in moments.

He woke the next morning ten minutes before his alarm, which was out of character for him. The run the previous night had invigorated him, and he felt much fresher and a lot less stressed than he had done in a long time.

He sat on the edge of his bed, trying to recollect if and what he had dreamt that night.

All he could remember was that he had dreamt of the run, except, in the dream, he hadn't stopped after a few minutes, he had kept going round and round, time after time. He recalled the people, none of whom he recognized, in spite of them feeling familiar, imploring him to stop. He also recalled calling back to them, by way of reply.

"Just one more time. I'm on the right track!"

He also spent some time considering his invisibility and why he had stayed that way for so long, and what he would do if this were to be a permanent fixture.

He knew exactly what he must do. Instead of worrying himself to distraction about what might happen, he decided he should just deal with what happened if, or when, it did happen. There was no use in trying to account for every single trivial variable, the vast majority of which were out of his control anyway. Thus resolved, he set off to go see Elizabeth and Jennifer.

Stood outside their apartment, he felt a pang of trepidation surge through him, and he found himself temporarily frozen to the spot, staring at the door. The realisation of what this meant was dawning on him. A flutter of butterflies cascaded through his abdomen. If he was still invisible, then, he felt, this could mean it *was* permanent, and he'd have a whole world of problems to figure out. This was not the time to waiver, he told himself. He must stay confident. He took a breath, raised his hand and knocked. A solid, determined knock, the knock of someone with purpose, one that the hearer wouldn't be able to doubt its purpose.

The door opened and he stood face to face with Jennifer.

The butterflies fluttered again.

Jennifer stared at him for a few seconds then leaned forward and looked outside the doorway.

"Elizabeth, did you hear someone knock?" she called back into the apartment.

"Yeah, I thought so." he heard Elizabeth call back. His heart sank. He hadn't changed.

Elizabeth's head came into view.

"Oh my God Jonathan!" she yelled.

A big, mischievous grin appeared on Jennifers face.

"Gotcha." she smirked, then leaned forward and gave him a big hug. "Good to have you back."

"You!" he said shaking his head in mock reproach, although, right at that moment, he could quite easily have murdered her. "I can't believe you could do that to me." He said, more seriously. But this is exactly what he would have expected her to do, he thought, a moment later, once the shock had subsided.

"So, how did you do it?" Jennifer asked when he'd sat down.

"I'm not sure." was his honest reply. "I nearly didn't sleep due to worrying about it. I ended up going for a run at about 1 a.m."

"A run?" she asked, somewhat surprised. "I didn't know you were a runner?"

"I'm not. I just had all this nervous energy built up and it was driving me mad. I couldn't sleep, and I didn't want to not sleep, that'd be guaranteed to keep me as I was, so I went for a run to tire myself out in the hope that it'd make me sleep. I might make a regular thing of it. I felt great this morning."

"Rather you than me." She replied, "but maybe that's it?"

"What? running?" he asked, a little baffled.

"No. Worrying." She replied. "Think about it. We had that run in at the takeaway. You said that was when you had the first dream that came true. Then the invisible thing when you did the thing with the movie and the mantra. I'm guessing that you were worrying about it working or whatever." she paused to allow him to consider her idea. "Then last night you were worrying about becoming visible. All your dreams are triggered by you worrying about something. What do you think?"

Jonathan sat back in the chair and thought about it for a good while.

He cast his mind back over events, replaying them in his mind trying to recollect how he had felt, emotionally, each time. So much had happened so far, but the emotional connection he'd had to each event seemed easier to recall than a lot of the other aspects.

She seemed to have a point. Every time he'd experienced a dream come to fruition, then the dream that he'd had, had been preconditioned by him worrying about it.

His thoughts started to run away with him as the ramifications of what this meant for his future started to hit home.

Were his dreams caused by his worries? If so, this would mean that, somehow, he needed to try control what he worried about and what played on his mind. If he was excited about something, then his dream may be a positive and beneficial one - and he could likely cope with those - but if he was scared, or angry about something, then who knows what manner of hell he could unleash on himself.

It then occurred to him that, so far, even the apparently good dreams had ended up being quite traumatising for him, as had happened when he became invisible. He thought this would have given him some fun but ended up being quite the nightmare. So now, not only would he need to control what he worried about, but even the seemingly good stuff had to be thought through to ensure he wasn't only considering the good outcomes, but also the not so good ones as well. And even the outright bad ones too, in order that it didn't turn out a complete disaster for him. This could prove the be quite catastrophic.

Could he spend the rest of his life trying to control every aspect of his mental faculties? for his own sanity, he would have to.

He truly had been cursed.

He voiced these thoughts to the girls, who listened intently.

"So," said Jennifer, thoughtfully. "In order to control these dreams, the ones that come to life, you need to, first off, give a full pro's and con's consideration to whatever is worrying you, and then, if it sounds like being an unbearable nightmare to live through, you have to find a way to not worry about it, so you don't dream it at all?"

"That sounds about right." he replied.

"...and that's presuming you even realise you're worrying about it?" interjected Elizabeth.

Jonathan and Jennifer both stared at her. She had a point; he wasn't always even aware he was worrying about some things. How could he deal with things in his subconscious?

"Is there any way you could just not dream?" asked Jennifer, only half joking. "Apparently, most people very rarely even dream," she continued, reading out some information she had found on the internet "and those that do, most don't even remember them anyway. What if you dream but don't remember it? how would you know that it's come to life?" she added, as an afterthought.

"I have no idea. That never even occurred to me. So far, I've only known the dreams that have come true because I remembered the dream itself, or felt a peculiar sense of Deja-vu. But I suppose I could have had dreams come to life that I've not remembered...I don't think I've any way of knowing, have I?" he replied, the dejected feeling consuming him now. It seems the odds were heavily stacked against him, and an overwhelming sense of futility darkened his horizons like an oncoming storm.

"Has anything happened to you that has just seemed outright weird?" asked Elizabeth, trying to be helpful. "Or just plain unbelievable?"

"I don't know. I've never thought of it that way. I mean weird things happen, right, but you don't think 'oh, hang on, did I dream that last night'. You just brush it off as weird and get on with your life." he replied, then, thinking a moment "And who's to say everyone dreams weird things? People must dream ordinary everyday events too, mustn't they?"

"Only if it's played on their mind though, right?" asked Elizabeth, trying to think of dreams that she had had in the past.

"Not necessarily. That just seems to be what causes mine, or rather, might be what causes mine. We don't know if other people dream about things they are worried about... I mean, do you?"

"Never even thought about it to be honest." she replied. "I mean, you don't do you. I'd be amazed if anybody had a dream and then woke up the next morning thinking 'oh, I wonder if I'm worrying about something?' "

"That's the point I'm making, sort of. I can only speak for what I feel, what I think and what happens to me, not what anyone else does. This is all so confusing anyway without adding in a million other variables."

"So... Are you saying we can't help you?" Jennifer asked, thoughtfully.

"Not at all. You help immensely."

"But you said adding in a million other variables makes it more confusing?"

"No. I said I can't speak for other people. But you can speak for what you think and feel. You can also empathise, as you have, with my situation and even though it hasn't necessarily happened to you, you can associate similar experiences you have had and extrapolate what you think pertinent for me to think about, which does help me...or can. Do you see?"

"I think so."

"Okay. Let's go back a step. You've already empathised with my situation, even though, to the best of your knowledge, you've never had a dream come to life. Right?"

"Absolutely."

"And you have had dreams, even though you cannot have had the exact same dream as me. Right?"

"Right."

"So, you *can* try to recall what *you* felt prior to having any of these dreams, to see if there are any similarities to mine. Right?"

"Yes." she replied as it finally sank in.

"So, you see, you are helping me." he said, reassuringly.

"That's good to know."

"Yes," interjected Jennifer, "but that doesn't tell us what you're going to do about it."

"It's a shame you can't just stop dreaming." said Elizabeth casually, repeating Jennifers earlier comment.

"If I knew how to do that, I wouldn't have a problem, would I?" Jonathan replied, a little more impatiently than he had intended. Elizabeth replied with a look of apology.

"But how did your dreams start to come true?" asked Jennifer. "that's what I don't understand. I mean, it's not exactly an everyday occurrence, is it? or we'd have already heard about it. It'd have been on the news or something."

"Hmm. I'm not so sure we would." replied Jonathan. "I mean, look how much trouble I've had with it. I'm not so sure there’s many people would want to broadcast that! I know I don't."

"No. True. But there must be things that everyone dreams about? right? Falling but never landing. Flying. Running but going nowhere. Being rich. That kind of thing?"

"But how would we know which rich people have dreamt it? I mean, most people become rich by working for it, or their families have. There's only really gamblers and lottery winners where it falls purely down to what could be called luck; and we would have no way of speaking to all the people who have won big on a bet, or won a lottery jackpot, in order for us to ask them if they'd dreamt about it happening beforehand. Nor if any of their other dreams had ever come true either.” He paused, and then, thinking further. “And even if they had, then would they remember if they had been worried about it prior? You see what I mean? too many parameters."

"But we don't have to." replied Jennifer. "You could. All you'd have to do is try to dream about winning the lotto, but without letting it play on your mind or worrying about it, and then see what happens. If it is how we think, then we'd have proved that its worrying about it that is the critical piece."

"Oh no!" replied Jonathan emphatically. "What if I did win? what then?"

"Er! then you'd be rich." Jennifer replied, as though he were an idiot for not knowing that. "How can that be bad?"

"I thought that about being invisible, and look how that turned out!" he replied. "No. I'd need to weigh up all the good and bad aspects about being rich." he replied. He was already trying to work it all out.

"You'd have lots of money and could do whatever you want. What could possibly be bad about that?"

"I don't know. Thats the point. I've never been rich, so I don't know what the bad parts of it are; and what is rich anyway? A million? ten million? a billion? Heck, I think someone is rich if they have a few hundred more than me, but I'm pretty sure that's not what makes someone 'rich'. Maybe I already am rich? there's going to be a lot of people out there with less than I have, right? ... Like I said about being invisible, my only ideas about that were the good stuff - the selfish bits that I wanted to get out of it. I never considered any of the aspects of it that could be bad, I had to figure those out when they happened, and they weren't good. I'd be stupid to think the same couldn't apply to suddenly becoming rich. I mean, have you ever been rich? how did you deal with it?" his speech becoming more panicked.

"No." replied Jennifer, realising the point. "I guess you're right I suppose."

"So, you see. I need to make sure I consider everything and make sure this also wouldn't turn out to be something we think is all good, when really, it's a bit good, but a whole lot of bad." he replied, more calmly now.

"Yeah. I guess so, when you put it like that."

"And before I start thinking about that, I have another problem to fix."

"Oh? and what's that?" Jennifer asked, a little surprised that he had more urgent things to think about.

"I'm not sure it's a good idea that I tell you." he replied evasively. She returned him a look that said 'oh! really?', so he decided to let them into the secret.

"You remember that folder I used so you could see me yesterday?"

"Yeah, what about it?"

"Well, that was the Professors notes for our next lecture that I kind of used my invisibility to steal."

Elizabeth and Jennifer's faces both bore an expression that was a combination of amusement and incredulity, in equal parts.

"You *stole* the professors lecture notes!" exclaimed Elizabeth. "Oh my God, Jonathan!"

"I didn't want to fall behind if the invisibility lasted longer, or stayed permanently. I didn't figure people would react too well to seeing my bag floating around the campus and into the lecture hall if I attended. So, I decided to get the notes, make my own copy and then fill in any blanks with you guys later on." he said apologetically, the sense of shame sitting heavily in his gut now.

"How did you get them?" Elizabeth asked

"I just followed him into his office. It's one of the good bits about being invisible, people don't see you. Then I just had to wait for him to leave the room for a short while so I could find them and take them. It was getting back to my apartment that was the difficult part. I had to go a long way out of the normal route. Hid behind trees. Behind dumpsters, and at one point, even dive over a wall into a snow drift. All to avoid anyone seeing that folder floating about..."

"And now you have to get it back, which, being visible now, will be just as hard." Elizabeth interrupted realising where he was going with this.

"Yes. I'm figuring it'll almost be the same problem, but in reverse. Carrying it about won't be difficult. I can shove it in my bag and go where I like. The hard part now is the bit that was easy before, and that is getting it back into his office without being seen."

"Unless you don't?" said Elizabeth in her usual ambivalent manner.

"What do you mean, 'unless you don't?'" he replied imitating her nonchalance.

"Exactly that. Why return it at all? surely, he must know it's gone by now? what difference would it make if you just binned them? as long as he never finds out who took them then what could he do?"

Jonathan thought about it. He looked at Elizabeth, then over to Jennifer and back to Elizabeth again.

"I'd feel too guilty." he finally said "and I don't want something like that on my mind. Who knows what I could end up dreaming? and what kind of trouble I'd end up in as a result. No, I need to know he has them back. That way I won't worry."

"Yeah, fair play. I forgot about that." she replied earnestly. "Is there any way you can get it back to him without having to go back to his office? Maybe just leave them somewhere he'd definitely find them?"

"Like where?"

"I dunno. What about the library?"

"Too busy." replied Jennifer. "Too many students, one of them might pick it up instead. Plus, I've never seen him in there. It'd at least have to be somewhere he goes."

"What about the lecture hall?" said Elizabeth. "We definitely know he goes in there, so he would definitely see it."

"Yeah, good idea." replied Jonathan, liking the simplicity. "But I'd still need to get in to put it there in the first place, and do it unseen. That would mean I'd have to do it just before a lecture. But wouldn't that mean he'd know someone in his class has taken them?"

"I think he'd already know someone in his class took them. Who else would? you'd just need to do it before a different lecture then." said Jennifer, suddenly getting an idea. "Sneak in before another lecture and let that professor find them and pass them back to him instead!? There's no way on earth they'd be able to track it back you then."

Jonathan nodded slowly, contemplating.

"Yeah. That could work. When's our next lecture?"

"Tomorrow morning." she replied.

"Right. So, if I can get it in tonight, I can place it on the desk at the front and he'll see it the following morning."

"Yes. And if we make sure we arrive after he does then there's even less chance of being suspected. It's perfect!"

"You two will have to come with me and keep a lookout though."

"Do we have to!?" asked Elizabeth. "I've never done anything illegal before."

"What are you talking about, illegal? We're returning property." said Jennifer.

"That was stolen! That we knew was stolen, and now we're going to break in to replace it."

"We're not breaking in, dummy. We're students at the University; we're allowed in there. We're not doing anything illegal."

"Still feels wrong." replied Elizabeth, sulkily. “I’m sure we're accessories or something."

"So, you're not going to help?" said Jennifer, who was beginning to become a little annoyed at Elizabeth.

"Of course, I am. I just feel... Bad, I guess" replied Elizabeth, a little sheepishly. She didn't like the idea of getting into trouble, but she also didn't like the idea of letting Jonathan down. She was conflicted. At high school she was amongst the most intelligent in her classes, and was ostracised because of it, and now she was at university, she had found herself struggling and Jonathan and Jennifer had accepted her for who she was and were the closest friends she had ever had. She didn't want to let them down.

They got to the lecture hall about ten minutes before the last lecture of the day was finishing, and they stood about outside the doors waiting for it to finish, looking as guilty as the criminals they felt they were. By the sounds of it, it was either Mathematics, or physics judging by the snippets they could hear, which was ideal for them as he didn't know anyone in his psychology class that did either maths or Physics, which meant that there would be no obvious suspects.

Suddenly, there was an explosion of noise followed, momentarily, by the doors crashing open as the students began pouring out, like a dam that had burst, its contents spilling out, uncontrollably.

He tried to peer inside to see if the lecturer was still there. She was. He could see her packing up her things and joining the flow of students that were exiting.

The moment she passed him, he quickly stepped inside the doorway, holding the door open to let the last of the students leave. He signalled to Jennifer, who was stood just outside the doorway, that he was going for it.

They had agreed that, whilst he was inside putting the folder somewhere, they would keep watch at the entrance, and, if anyone looked to be returning to the lecture hall, they would bang on the door to let him know.

Thankfully, no-one did. The advantage of the afternoon lectures being that people rarely hung around afterwards. Not that many wanted to hang around after the morning ones either.

Jonathan slipped back out into the corridor and the three of them joined the throng of traffic that was walking up and down the corridor, merging into the flow of students like the man of the crowd of Edgar Allen Poe's story. The anonymity they wished for provided, unknowingly, by the ignorant masses.

Fifteen minutes later, they were sat in the coffee shop in silence.

"Is no-one going to say anything?" asked Jennifer quietly. Elizabeth shot her a nervous glance.

"You're right. We need to act normal." replied Jonathan, just as quietly.

"Why?" asked Jennifer. "Literally no-one knows what we've done. Why would anyone be paying any attention to us to begin with? we're just three people sat in a coffee shop."

"Okay." conceded Jonathan "but we at least need to try not look quite so guilty. It'll make people suspicious." He got her point though. It was only their own paranoia making them feel, and act, suspiciously. All they really needed to do was forget about the last hour and just say and do the kinds of things they normally did.

"So... What should we talk about?" he asked, after a few more minutes of silence and them looking at each other.

Both Elizabeth and Jennifer opened their mouths to say something, looked thoughtful for a second, then closed them without speaking, and looked back at Jonathan. The three of them sat in silence until they had finished their drinks.

"Come on. Let’s go back to mine to study." said Jonathan, louder now, and emphasising the word 'study' hoping the girls would take the hint that he really meant 'talk about what they had done where others couldn't hear them.'

"I can't help it. I still feel nervous." said Elizabeth when they were back at Jonathan’s apartment and were going over the events. “Are you sure they won't be able to link this back to the three of us?"

"You're blowing this out of all proportion.” said Jennifer. "He hasn't murdered anyone. We haven't helped him get away with anything serious. He just took some papers from the Professor, and we helped him to make sure they were returned to sender."

"Oh my god!" exclaimed Jonathan in alarm "We could have done that!"

"Done what?" asked Elizabeth confused.

"Posted them back. It would have been way easier, and safer." replied Jonathan. "Why didn't I think of that before!?"

The penny dropped for both Elizabeth and Jennifer instantaneously, and they couldn't help but find the revelation somewhat risible. They began laughing, at first to themselves, then out loud, at the absurd and convoluted way the three of them had made sure they got the papers back to the professor anonymously.

"For three University Students, we sure can be dumb at times." Jennifer said, still laughing, and this set them off laughing all the more. All the tension, paranoia and stress, alleviated in one tidal wave of emotional release. It helped them all put the event behind them, which Jonathan was most grateful for, as the repercussions could have been far more severe for him. He had no idea what torments his dream would have unleashed on him with the weight of this kind of worry bearing on him.

Chapter XII

Jonathan couldn't sleep. The arms of Morpheus failed to embrace him, so he lay awake, twisting and turning from one side to the other, restlessly.

The truth of it was that he was scared to sleep. He knew that. Should he sleep he had little, if any, control over whether he dreamt or not, and, if he did dream, he then, correspondingly, had no control over *what* he would dream. There was every chance that he might dream about things that were playing on his mind, either good or bad; and, to make matters worse, he wasn't conscious of having anything overtly concerning on his mind, aside from sleep itself, which made the situation all the more dangerous. He already knew that things that seemed superficially good, could also have a great deal of negative connotations that he was unlikely to have considered. All these thoughts rolled around his mind relentlessly. Not so much rolled, as careered, crashed and collided, like the balls on a pool table after an aggressive break off. He simply needed to find a way to avoid dreaming. Easier said than done, naturally. Though, until he could do that, he would have to try make do with not sleeping at all. Climbing out of bed, he made a cup of coffee, using a tablespoon full of coffee granules, and gave the matter some further consideration.

Coffee made, he made himself comfortable, sprawling out on the couch, and let the avalanche of thoughts in his head settle, so that he might begin to organise some type of order to them and, hopefully, formulate a logical solution for each.

He took a sip of the hot coffee; it was strong, very strong, and very bitter. It made his mouth do funny things involuntarily. The bitterness of it, or maybe just the reaction to the harsh taste, gave him an immediate kick. He wasn't used to having his coffee unsweetened, but he thought the benefits of the caffeine would outweigh the taste aspect. He had heard of students using amphetamine so that they could stay awake and cram for exams, but he had also heard bad stories about after-effects, and he really wasn't prepared to venture down that avenue if he could at all avoid it.

Not least because he wasn't searching for a temporary fix, but for something that could, potentially, become a permanent fixture in his life. He had no idea how long his condition would affect him, after all.

He meditated on that point for a while and shuddered. The thought of, somehow, never sleeping again, filled him with a fear that vibrated right to his very core. He had heard stories of sleep deprivation experiments that had left the people both physically and psychologically damaged, permanently.

He recalled some of the pictures to his mind. No, he needed to find some way of having a dreamless sleep.

'To sleep, perchance to not dream' he thought to himself, smirking at his pseudo-Shakespearean misquote. But it was a valid point, how to sleep without dreaming. That was a question he seriously needed an answer to. How do you do something and avoid what is a definite, viable, but seemingly random, consequence? That was the problem that he now dedicated his entire focus on solving.

He tried to think back through his life to any time he could recall being asleep and not dreaming.

An impossible and futile task.

He had rarely ever even considered his dreams before, never mind thought about not dreaming them. It was a natural component of a human's nocturnal activities. One that almost everyone took for granted, to such an extent that, equally, they also must never pay the slightest regard to them either. Unless they were particularly spectacular - and even then, he suspected no-one thought of them for too long after the event.

Many a night's sleep that he'd had, had been dreamless, or possibly just so unremarkable that they went unremembered, immediately forgettable. He tried to think shorter term, the last month or so before he'd noticed them coming to life, and he guessed that, in all actuality he only dreamt maybe once or twice per week that he could reasonably recall with any level of certainty.

Once or twice a week. He thought about those odds for a while. Given his condition, that was still too many.

By now, the coffee had cooled down sufficiently enough for him to drink it in one, gag-reflex inducing motion. He did so, the need of the caffeine fix to wake him proving too great. He then spent the next few minutes gipping, trying not to vomit the contents of the mug straight back up again. His bowels complained about the sudden bolus as well, and he quickly made haste to the bathroom.

Sat on the toilet, he wondered how long it would take the caffeine to kick in. Not fast enough as far as he was concerned, he could feel the tiredness making its presence known, his eyelids starting to feel heavy.

He went back to contemplating his problem while he waited. He needed to try simplifying the situation.

As far as he could rationalise; as he was unable to completely control how his dreams manifested, he had only two options, possibly three. The first being to not sleep. This posed the obvious further problem around sleep deprivation and its consequences, as well as it being unsustainable. The second option was to find a way to sleep, but without dreaming, which was the problem he was setting his focus on now.

It was while contemplating this very thing, that an idea occurred to him. Granted, it wasn't a particularly enticing idea, but it was at least something. He thought hard. He wanted to be quite sure that his memory was not failing him, or at the very least, that he wasn’t misremembering a conceivable thing that only might have happened, considering what it was.

The cogitation ran as follows. He had been trying to recollect instances in his past, where he had been asleep, but knew he had not dreamed. This was not the easiest of situations to recall to a conscious state of memory, as he was absolutely certain that many nights absence of dreaming, he could simply put down to them just being instantly forgotten about, which did not guarantee, absolutely, that he had not dreamed.

He needed to sieve through these occasions and allow them to fall through so that he could disregard them entirely. Hoping that what then remained were the times whereby they fit into the parameters of his requirements. He could not allow any assumptions to be left, he needed one hundred percent certainty. He knew it was there, somewhere, he'd had that strange feeling of something, deep in the recesses of his mind, that there was something, but he was struggling to get close enough to grab at it.

He was distracted, at this point, by the caffeine kicking in. Sweat broke out on his brow, and beads began to trickle down his forehead and temples, at the same time as a violent bowel movement thundered through his colon, like a mass of rats, excessively eager to return to their sewer.

This, inadvertently, provided him with just the distraction he needed; well, maybe not 'just' the distraction, but it gave him *a* distraction, and, like a lightbulb switching on suddenly, his subconscious mind finished off solving the puzzle, and there it was.

On a couple of occasions, he had been asleep - of sorts - and not dreamt. He had been in accidents that had left him unconscious.

He knew of the accidents only because he had been told of them afterwards, but on each occasion, he had been unconscious, without any recollection of dreaming, for an unknown period of time. He couldn't recall on these occasions the actual accident, nor being in an ambulance. He remembered a fraction before the accident, and then waking up in a hospital bed. He drew the conclusion, one which he was adamant of, that being concussed, and unconscious gave him dreamless sleep...but for how long. He tried to estimate how much time passed from his accident to him coming round on the hospital ward. An hour, maybe two.

This led him to another consideration, now he had begun to think about hospitals. It occurred to him that another time he'd had dreamless sleep was when he was in surgery and under general anaesthetic. He'd been unconscious without dreams for several hours under those circumstances. There were a few obvious problems with that approach, however.

Bowels now stable, he cleaned himself up and returned to the living room to continue his thoughts.

His final option was to alternate these approaches. A night or maybe two of not sleeping alternated with a night, or maybe two, of dreamless sleep - if he could find a way.

He needed to organise his thoughts, so he got his notepad out, and on three separate pages, wrote out an option at the top, drew a line down the middle of the page and wrote Pro and Con at the top of each column.

After lengthy searches on the computer around amphetamine use, general anaesthetic and being rendered unconscious repeatedly, he found this gave his con's columns a distinctly longer list, all of which were of no small concern, than the pro's columns, which were limited to either 'achieves a dreamless sleep' or ' do not sleep' with nothing else.

He re-read the Cons columns two or three more times and then wrote in the Pro's column 'I'm desperate!!'

To purchase a regular supply of the amphetamines and benzodiazepines would cost him money. He had no idea how much they cost, nor did he even know where to obtain them from, but he figured there had to be someone at the University who could point him in the right direction, after all he'd heard of students using amphetamines so they could cram for exams, so it fell, logically, that someone must sell them, and if they sold amphetamines, surely they must be able to get hold of sedatives as well.

First of all, of course, he needed the money, which got him to thinking about Jennifers suggestion, to dream himself rich.

Chapter XIII

Jonathan woke with a start.

'What time is it? ... How long have I been asleep? ...asleep! Ohmygod! didIdream? whatdidIdream? Think! Think!'

These thoughts flashed through his mind at lightning speed, one uninterrupted stream of semi-conscious dread.

Panic rose inside him, quickly, paralysing him. He didn't know what to do next. A pain demanded his attention as he raised his head. His neck ached from the unusual position in which he had fallen asleep in the chair. He rubbed the back of his neck and slowly, and ever so slightly, moved his head from side to side, then from left to right, trying to loosen it up. It felt as though he had been hung and his neck needed to crack back into place. He stood and stretched out the tightness from his body, arms high above his head, fingers interlocking 'Kkr, Kkr' as the joints cracked. He then turned his head as far as he could to one side, place one palm under his jaw and the other on the opposite temple, and pushed sharply. 'Kkrr' as his neck cracked. He turned his head to other direction and repeated the process, a single, but louder 'Kok'. He felt better almost instantly.

Neck pain now subsided; he could turn his mind back to his initial problem. He checked the time, Six forty-eight. He'd been asleep for about three hours or so. Was that enough for him to sleep? He tried to recall any dreams, but his head was feeling thick, and he was groggy from such a short night's sleep. He went to get himself a glass of water while he thought.

He had a terrifying feeling that he had dreamt, but he simply could not remember any of it. It haunted him with faint echoes of conversations; but they were distant and devoid of actual images. Like whispered conversations held in the furthest corners of a darkened room. The pitch blackness absorbing any of the volume.

Jonathan sat at the kitchen table with his head in his hands. He was certain he had dreamed, but he had no idea what. Regret, fear and self-pity all welled up in his gut and tears slowly began to run down his cheeks. Why was he cursed in this way? and what disaster was he now going to find himself in when it finally manifested into reality ... And how would he even know?

The walk to the university building wasn't ordinarily a long one, especially as he typically met up with Elizabeth and Jennifer somewhere along the way - usually outside the entrance to his apartment block - and the ensuing conversations occupied them and made the time fly.

Today seemed to be an exception.

The first sight that came to him on exiting the apartment block, was not Elizabeth, nor was it Jennifer. Instead, it was Josh and his friends. They looked in his direction, and he swallowed, hard, trying to push down the palpable fear that he was now feeling. He had no idea what plans they were concocting to torment him, but, this time, they said nothing. Josh didn't take his eyes off him though.

A paralysing sense of foreboding crept through Jonathan; he would much prefer Josh to actually do something. This sense, that something would happen, but that he didn't know either what, nor when, was proving to be torturous. He wanted to run, get as far away as he possibly could, and as quickly as he possibly could, but he couldn't make his legs obey.

Josh made a move to towards him, this was all he needed. The surge of adrenaline that pulsed through him when his overactive imagination flashed through images of all the conceivable tortures Josh could inflict on him broke the spell. He turned and set off running to find an alternative route to go meet the girls, as fast as he possibly could.

After a few minutes, he slowed to check if Josh was following, and, on seeing that he wasn't, he stopped and caught his breath.

He could see the girls just up ahead and he smoothed himself down so as not to look quite so dishevelled, before approaching.

"Hey, how are you doing?" Elizabeth asked, nonchalantly.

"Fine." he replied. A typical reply that people gave when they really meant something a great deal more, but either couldn't be bothered to explain, didn't know where to start, or they thought the person asking wouldn't really care.

In this case, however, it was because they were out in public, and he couldn't risk others overhearing them.

When he was certain that they had a little more privacy, he gave a more honest answer. He had no idea how to caress it into the conversation they were having at the time, so he just blurted it out.

He began by trying to explain his plan, but suddenly paused when he felt an earie sense of claustrophobia. This was compounded by an equally unnerving sense that they were being listened in on. He looked around and there behind them he could see Josh approaching, several meters away, but getting closer. Jonathan shivered at the feeling that he had sensed him approach, but what made him shiver, was more than that, it was the tentacles of fear, crawling, icily down his spine.

The terror he had felt before rose in him once again. As though that icy feeling had hit the bottom of his spine stopped, turned and begun working its way back up, transforming from simple fear to abject terror on its returning journey. His stomach clenched. Josh wouldn't attack him here, would he? Not with so many witnesses around. No, surely not! He'd be risking too much; assaulting another student, in front of witnesses would get him arrested and kicked out of university. He might be a bully, but he wasn't that dumb, was he?

Feeling the increased sense of security that crowds provided, Jonathan returned his attention back to the girls and quietly continued to tell them how he planned to alternate sleepless nights with dreamless sleep, or, at least, so he hoped, until he could figure out either something more permanent, or until he knew just how long this curse would last. But, as both necessitated pharmaceutical assistance, he needed to find someone who he could obtain them from.

They were both very dubious of this plan, and made themselves perfectly clear on the matter.

"I don't know about this." said Elizabeth "drugs! what if you get addicted?"

"I don't see I have..." he began.

"And what are the side effects of these drugs?" Jennifer interjected, before he could finish. "One's an upper, the other a downer. It can't be healthy to be mixing them? what's that going to do to your body? to your mind?"

"I don't know." he replied " but, as I was saying, I don't think I have any other options. I can't control these dreams, not fully anyway, and no matter how good you think they are going to be, these dreams always end up a great deal more problematic; and who knows how much worse they *could* get? I can't keep living in fear of my dreams coming true. I just can't."

"But there *must* be something else," replied Elizabeth, imploringly. "There must! There just has to be."

"Which is what, exactly? The only other option I could think of was to knock myself out, but the very real risk of that is brain damage, and I don't think even that would stop me dreaming. In fact, I suspect it would just stop me being able to do anything about the dreams when they did come to life. So, at least this way I still have some semblance of control."

They listened to what he said, still unconvinced, but they took it on board and considered it, along with vainly trying to think of a safer alternative.

As it was, they couldn't, and so, regretfully, they had to concede the point. Whichever option he took there seemed to be problems to face.

"I need the loo." said Jennifer suddenly after a few minutes. "Come on Elizabeth."

It seemed rather obvious it wasn't the toilet she wanted, but a private conversation that most definitely did not involve Jonathan himself.

"You wait here." she said to Jonathan as she grabbed Elizabeth and dragged her away.

Less than five seconds after they had disappeared, a quiet voice appeared from over his left shoulder.

"I can help you with that."

It was Josh, who was stood, rather menacingly it seemed to Jonathan, at his shoulder. He started a little, he couldn't help himself, and he turned to face him. A cold fear ran down his spine. He wanted to run, but his body wouldn't respond. Despite every rational part of his brain telling him to flee, there was something in Josh's eyes that had him captivated. He knew how rabbits felt when they saw the headlights. He was overtly conscious that the crowds that had once surrounded them all, had now thinned considerably, leaving the two of them quite alone. The voice in the back of his head was screaming that something very painful was about to happen to him, but those eyes kept him rooted to the spot.

"Wh-Wha-wha?" he stammered, cowering a step backwards, away from the threat. Josh looked back at him as though he were mentally deficient. Couldn't he remember his own conversation from just a moment ago?

"I said, I can help you with that." he repeated quietly, but more firmly, looking around to make sure he wasn't being overheard. He'd been listening into Jonathan's conversation himself, so he knew how easy it was to hear what was being said.

"Whwhwith what?" Jonathan was still full of terror, Josh seemed considerably larger than he had realised, and his presence so close to him was insanely intimidating.

"With what you need." Josh whispered back, the tone in his voice making it evident he was losing his patience.

Jonathan continued to stare at him, fear written all over his face.

"Drugs." whispered Josh, raising his eyebrows in a 'you understand?' kind of way "What do you need?"

The relief Jonathan felt at the moment of realisation that he wasn't about to be beaten to a pulp by Josh, but actually helped, was so overwhelming he nearly lost control of his bowels.

Thankfully, he managed to contain himself and merely let out a belch of a laugh, that just as quickly he stifled. He was about to procure illicit substances, and it wasn't really a laughing matter. Plus, Jonathan had a deep rooted and innate mistrust of Josh, viewing him as his nemesis, especially when he considered the events of the last few weeks. It confused him that his nemesis should now turn out to possibly become his greatest friend in his time of need, but his desperation overrode his common sense.

"Diazepam." Jonathan said, as casually as he could bring himself to, yet, in spite of intending to sound calm and confident, he heard his own voice almost squeak the word. It sounded like he was going through puberty all over again, his voice rising and falling uncontrollably. "And amphetamine." His confidence evaporated as he said this, he couldn't even look Josh in the eyes anymore. He felt like a naughty school child, the shame rising like a tidal wave in his guts. He had expected his first purchase to be a little nerve wracking, but he also figured he'd have to get over it as this may end up a regular transaction. He hadn't counted on his sworn enemy being the vendor though.

"Yeah, no problem." said Josh very calmly. 'Now that's the calmness I wanted to speak like' thought Jonathan 'he's clearly done this a few times before'.

"How much do you need?"

Jonathan's mind went blank, he hadn't thought about that. He'd never taken either of these before and had no idea how they would affect him. He didn't want to buy too many in case they didn't work as expected, but, in the same vein, he didn't want to have to keep coming back too often either, not to Josh.

"Thirty...of each." he replied. He calculated that if he was going to alternate them that this should give him a couple of months supply.

"You want thirty amphetamines?" Josh asked, as though Jonathan had just asked for thirty armadillos.

"Err...tablets?...Yes. Please!" replied Jonathan, his nervousness showing, and his doubts growing.

"Ohh." replied Josh suddenly understanding what Jonathan was meaning. "You want some F and H?! ... You having a little nerd party, eh?" and he winked knowingly at Jonathan, then seeing the look on his face, said "You nerds don't party, do you? You cramming for an exam or something?"

Jonathan had heard about F and H, short for Focused and happy; rumour had it that one of the chemistry majors was making his own stimulants to help him study for lengthy periods of time, over twelve hours the rumour went, and that he'd begun to sell it as a way to help finance his way through university.

Jonathan had always believed this to be just an urban legend, 'impoverished Chemistry student resorts to making his own drugs to pay his way through Uni', it just sounded like the kind of story he thought would be spread round most campuses, but now, here he was, being offered a mysterious drug manufactured by an impoverished Chemistry student. Any hesitation he'd had was swamped by the idea of being able to stay awake and alert for twelve hours at a time.

"Err, hmm, yes." he replied quietly, feeling as though the whole University could now hear his conversation and were suddenly all listening in.

"Okay, let's see, thirty diazepam, thirty F&H's..." Josh looked at Jonathan as though weighing him up. "Three hundred. When do you want them?"

'Three hundred!' Jonathan thought. That seemed a lot of money. He cursed himself for not finding out what they should cost, beforehand. He had no idea if this was a fair price or whether he was being ripped off. But he was desperate, and he didn't have many other options, so he agreed.

"Okay." he said, nodding as though he thought this a fair price. "As soon as really, when can you get them?"

"Give me an hour. I'll meet you back here."

An hour! Jonathan was under the impression he'd have a day or two to get the money together, he didn't expect to be dealt with so quickly. Part of him was impressed by the efficiency. He looked at his watch. His lecture was starting in ten minutes, and he'd need to go to the bank for the money, so he agreed to meet Josh back here at lunch time.

The entire lecture was a waste of time. Jonathan was so distracted that he was unable to take anything on board. He just stared at the wall above the lecturer's head, and let his mind torment him with everything that he could conceivably, and inconceivably, think of going wrong. All of which were, by and large, completely irrational.

First, he was convinced that this was some elaborate ploy by Josh and his friends to get him alone and beat him up - he would have a reasonable amount of cash on him, after all - or even kidnap him, take him somewhere remote and torture him, even to death.

Then he considered that Josh might be some kind of undercover police officer. Was he going to arrest him for buying illicit substances, and would he end up in prison for the rest of his life?

He managed to talk, or rather think, himself out of this ridiculous scenario by deint of reasoning that it would constitute some level of entrapment. Josh had been the one to offer him the drugs. But that train of thought stuck in his mind and morphed from Josh being a police officer, to him formulating some devious ploy where all the students in his year were laying hidden, and at some pre-arranged signal from Josh, they would all leap out from their hiding places and laugh at his desperation, ridiculing him mercilessly, and that he would feel so ashamed at himself that he would lock himself in his apartment, too humiliated to step foot outside, and he would end up starving to death because his friends would abandon him and he wouldn't even be able to go do any shopping.

His eyes began to shift around the lecture hall. He was frantically looking for any signs that any of them could be involved in his paranoic collusion. Did that guy just look at him? Did she just snigger at him? what was she laughing about? What did they know?

Jonathan desperately needed to get a grip. His paranoia was getting out of control. He risked driving himself insane.

None of these things were going to happen, he tried to tell himself, attempting to force some semblance of objective rationality into proceedings. All he was doing, was going to buy some things from someone who had them to sell, and who wanted to earn themselves some money. It was that simple, so what if it was his enemy that was selling it.

So why could he not rid himself of the nerve shredding fear that it was, of all people, Josh who was coming to his aid?

His self-inflicted mental torture was interrupted by movement. The rest of the classroom were beginning to pack their things away and starting to file out of the auditorium.

Jonathan paused for a few minutes, staying stationary in his seat, allowing the rest of the students to file out first. When there were only a half dozen stragglers dithering behind, he packed his things away as well, and left as briskly as he could.

After a brief diversion, via the bank, he made his way to meet Josh. He tried to rehearse how the transaction might go, so that he could appear as natural, and confident, as possible. But with each iteration of the conversation that he imagined, he found himself feeling more and more uncertain. Was that really how drug dealers actually spoke to their customers? it didn't feel right, didn't feel casual. But then, he had never been in this situation before, so he had no idea what 'right' felt like.

The closer he got to the meeting place, the more nervous he became, if that was even possible. He'd been a bundle of nerves for the last hour or so. The doubts started to overload his mind, turning his innards to jelly.

Was he doing the right thing here? Was this all a big mistake? Did he actually have a choice, *really* have a choice? Had he just decided he didn't because he couldn't think the whole thing through fully?

Then he saw Josh up ahead, and his brain froze.

Even from this distancer, Josh looked enormous, bigger than he had ever remembered him being, and he remembered him being big! Was his mind playing tricks on him? Was this just some strange optical illusion?

Josh saw him approaching and gave him a nod of acknowledgement in response. The closer Jonathan got to him; the bigger Josh seemed to look. By the time he got next to him, he seemed to be seven feet tall, and almost as wide.

"You got the money?"

Jonathan held out the cash. Josh took it, counting it quickly, then passed over two small bags containing the pills.

Jonathan was so frightened that he didn't even look at them, he just shoved his hands in his coat pockets, turned and walked away as fast as he could, grateful that the encounter was finally as an end. His heart was palpitating all the way back to his apartment.

And as simple as that, it was done.

Chapter XIV

Jonathan sat at the kitchen table, staring. He was staring at two small bags full of pills. One containing F and H, the other diazepam.

He'd had a nerve-wracking day, more so after he had made his purchase, as this then meant he was walking around with both bags on his person all afternoon. The sense of guilt unrelentingly eating away at him. All the time, a nervous twitchiness building inside him, thinking the police were about to close in and arrest him. Paranoia not only making him suspicious they were following him in plain clothes, but that everyone he saw was part of some conspiracy to apprehend him. Every sound made him jump. He didn't think his heart would hold out. By the time he'd got back to his apartment he was perspiring from the nerves.

That abject fear didn't begin to subside until more than an hour after he had closed the door behind him, so certain was he that some kind of task force was about to kick open his door, just like he'd seen happen on television.

By the time two hours of waiting - for what he thought was the inevitable - had passed, he finally began to settle. He then gave them another fifteen minutes to barge in the door. When they hadn't, he sat at the table, took a few deep controlled breaths to calm himself, retrieved the bags from his pocket and sat staring at them. He couldn't believe he had actually done it. He'd *actually* bought drugs. For the first time in his life. It was a strange thing for him to feel proud of himself for.

He looked from bag to bag and back again. The size, shape and colour of them were different, which, he thought, was a good thing, as it made it harder for him to get them out of order. The diazepam were small, round, creamy white coloured tablets scored down the middle on one side, smooth and plain on the other, whereas the F and H were pink, about the same size, but instead of a score down the centre they had a semi-colon and closed bracket on them, which, when turned ninety degrees looked like a smiley face winking at him. An indication of what to expect, he presumed. He'd heard of F and H before, months ago. There had been a spate of news reports of nightclub goers dying from its use, which made him all the more nervous, but on doing his original investigations into them, and their side effects, he had found that you could mitigate the worst effects by drinking plenty of water so as to avoid dehydration. Nevertheless, that did little to alleviate the profound trepidation he felt.

His eyelids were feeling heavy. The stress of the day, combined with the fact that the adrenaline was now starting to wear off, further combined with the little sleep he'd had the night before, was now, rapidly catching up on him and he was now slipping into 'tired-baby' territory, his head nodding forwards as he began slipping into a somnolent blanket, only to be wrenched back into wakefulness by the sudden jerk of his head falling forward.

His original plan had been to take a diazepam tonight to try catch up on some of the rest he'd missed out on the day before, but as it was only half past six, he decided it was too early for sleep and thought it better to try stay awake for a few more hours yet. He turned on his computer and began making himself another cup of coffee while he waited for it to boot up.

He didn't trust a regular cup of enough to keep him awake long enough, so he prepared another of his outrageously strong cups, like he's made before, and placed two tablespoons of coffee into a mug, added four sweeteners to combat the bitterness, and then half-filled the mug with warm water. The strong, bitter smell hit his olfactory system with a kick, that made him blink a couple of times, as he stirred. It was strong enough to bend iron, almost sludgy, as it swirled around the mug, and he knew this was not going to be easy to drink. He'd purposely stopped the kettle well short of boiling, so he'd be able to drink it quicker. The more he had to wait, the less likely he would be of actually drinking it, and he was too tired to wait for it to have cooled enough.

He took the mug across to his computer, opened up a blank WORD document and adjusted the brightness of the screen to the maximum setting, which was slightly painful to look at. He knocked back the coffee, downing it in two horrifically bitter gulps. His teeth felt as though they were contracting themselves away from the awful taste, and a fraction of a second later his stomach also revolted against the sudden onslaught, spasming and causing him to retch, quite violently a few times. Jonathan was making a concerted and valiant effort in the battle he was in with his stomach, which was trying to reject its latest addition. He took a couple of careful breaths and went back to the kitchen to swill his mouth out with water.

The worst of the taste now removed from his mouth he went back and sat at the monitor and stared at the ultra-bright screen. The effect this was all having on his brain was shocking. The opposing effects of the exhaustion he felt, and the hyper stimulation of the coffee, combined with the brilliantly bright screen, collided with each other like a raging storm crashing against a cliff face, the result being that not only did he want to vomit, but his heart was racing, even though his head was still adamant that it wanted to sleep. He could feel the beginnings of a headache coming on.

He was already regretting his choice of action, the brightness of the screen was too much for him, so he turned it down, back to normal and closed WORD, opening up YouTube instead, he'd watch some music videos and hope the combination of sound and light would have a better effect of keeping him awake and alert.

His stomach began to bubble as the coffee worked its way through his intestines, and the response was identical to the previous occasion, only this time he felt he had a great deal less chance of controlling it and no amount of clenching would prevent the inevitable.

Panic exploded through his mind. He leapt up from his desk and paced across the apartment to the bathroom as quickly as he could, crashing the door open so hard the handle embedded itself in the wall, where it stuck fast.

Several very uncomfortable minutes later, the intestinal tsunami had abated, and he sat, with his sweat drenched head in his hands, cursing himself for not remembering the first occasion that he had made this identical mistake; but he was also quietly thankful that, now he had the pills, he would not have to resort to this drastic measure in the future.

After waiting a sufficient period of time to ensure there were to be no repeat episodes, he washed up and returned back to his computer to continue watching music videos.

The stimulatory effects of the coffee and music seemed to be winning the battle, at last, but an hour later, the balance was tipping back in the favour of fatigue, and he began to notice his eyes feeling heavy, and his head began to dip forward again.

He looked at the clock, five to eight. He had fought the tiredness as long as he felt he could. Filling a glass with water, he put a diazepam on the tip of his tongue and swigged the glass in one hit. The coolness of the water helping to wash away the remnants of the bitter coffee aftertaste and settle his stomach a little.

He took a warm shower as he waited for the drug to start working, he'd forgotten to look into how long it took for it to take effect, so, showered and dried, he lay face down on the bed and waited for the sleep to come.

A blanket of blackness washed over him without him even realising.

* * * *

Faint muffled sounds rapidly became more coherent background noise. The sensation he was present followed soon after, the blackness changing to a dark grey and then a pinkish grey as the light made its presence known.

He opened his eyes.

The first thing he was aware of was that the bed covers against his cheek were wet. The next thing was the feeling of calmness. At that precise moment not one single care in the world troubled him. He felt he could lie here for an eternity, the soft comfort of the bed covers hugging him, as though to remind him that the universe is now protecting him, from everything.

He hadn't felt so carefree in a long time.

He rose and looked for the clock. It felt like he had only nodded off a short while ago, maybe half an hour, but the clock told a different story. It was now just after eight a.m. He'd been asleep for around twelve hours. He checked the clock again in case his mind was playing tricks, but it merely reiterated its original statement. His body seemed to confirm it as well; he felt the heaviness of body that came as a result of a long night's sleep.

The sense of calmness - which bordered on the euphoric - stayed with him most of the morning, but the freshness of the twelve-hour sleep stayed until late into the evening. But, as ten p.m. began to approach, even that began to fade and both body and mind gave way to a tide of fatigue that was gently washing over it, like the sea encroaches onto the beach of an evening, almost unnoticed, except to those paying particular attention. Which Jonathan was.

When he felt the fatigue building to a point of dominating his wakefulness, he began to make preparations for that day's strategy. This time, he placed one of the pink pills on the tip of his tongue and washed it down with a glass full of water. He refilled the glass and went and sat at the computer while he waited for it to take effect.

As it was with the diazepam the night before, so it was with the F and H tonight - in so far as he had no idea how long it would take to take effect, nor what the actual effect would be on him. But that didn't matter, the YouTube video that was playing had his full attention. He wasn't, ordinarily, a huge fan of classical music. He could listen to it, as background music. He found it soothing when he was studying, but he would never go out and actually buy it.

What he was listening to now, was blowing his mind. Someone had made a video of some orchestral music, Mendelssohn it said, and combined it with a slide show of some especially beautiful scenery that seemed to captivate his very soul.

He smiled inanely at the sheer beauty, staring wide-eyed as one scene, then another, came on screen.

Each scene made him feel as though he were a God, connecting with nature herself. Never had Jonathan experienced anything so sublime. His soul peaked and troughed in time with the music, his very being perfectly synchronised, higher and higher he seemed to rise, each peak lifting him to a new level, each trough, higher still than the predecessor. Each wave transcending him to newer heights. He felt like a feather, caught in a warm draft, a cushion of air lifting him gently, all on the back of the musical notes. Never had he felt so happy, it made him feel like sending a message to the supreme creator, telling them what a wonderful, beautiful, being they were for such a magnanimous gift, to share this masterpiece with humanity, and that he loved them, from the very top to the very bottom of his soul, for doing so.

When that video finished, Jonathan sat back in his chair exhilarated. Riding the crest of the wave of euphoria he was on. This was incredible. He felt so connected to the universe he could feel natures fingers run along the length of his gums, making his mouth stretch and contract in time with their caresses.

He sucked his teeth, wanting to taste her touch.

His heart raced; he needed more music. He wanted to dance, to communicate the unfettered love and adoration he felt, back to her. He knew just the song, quickly typing it into the search bar and playing the first entry that returned. The beat kicked in and his soul catapulted into the stratosphere at the joy of the sound. He leapt to the centre of the room and started to dance, spinning round, just like the song said. It's pulse moving him like a marionette.

Each time a song finished, he typed in another one and carried on dancing. He had never enjoyed himself so much in his entire life. He loved the music, he loved the computer, he loved his apartment, the University, the city, the country, Everyone.

He loved everything!!

After what seemed like no time at all, Jonathan let the song finish and sat down. He was sweating profusely, but still the need to dance was with him. He looked at his watch, it was five a.m. now. Where had the time gone!? He remembered that he needed to drink plenty of water, so grabbed a glass of, drank it down compulsively, then had another, and then a third.

He went and sat on the couch, laughing at nothing in particular.

* * * *

The next couple of weeks were the strangest Jonathan had ever experienced. The first few days were not so bad, although he felt decidedly rough the day after taking F and H, a feeling compounded by the fact that, while initially the best days, they were soon transformed once the drug had worn off, into the most intolerably long, and, by comparison, miserable days.

Butterfly days, he began to refer to them as. Two halves of the same, opened out into a mirror image of one another, only one half was joyous, sweet, tasty, and sadly short lived.

The other, misery, sour and drawn out, seconds seeming to last minutes, minutes lasting hours.

It didn't take long for the effects of the sleeping tablets to become woefully inadequate. The dreamless sleep, while a relief in one regard, made those days feel even shorter, and, although that brought the F and H - what a perfect name for the drug, he thought - it also brought the eternal damnation day with it. The days in which his feelings of abject misery seemed unassailable. Until the next time, which, somehow, seemed to take the misery of the last occasion as a challenge that it must, and often did, surpass.

Then, in his more lucid moments, he began to notice that he felt decidedly more sluggish, almost drunken, for the better part of the morning after. Not the histrionic drunkenness often seen in movies - that people found amusing - but the more real drunkenness of a high functioning alcoholic who tried to keep a sense of normality to their drunken state.

He also began noticing that he was slurring his words a little, had a faint lack of coordination which was accompanied by absent mindedness. He was also, more and more frequently, finding himself staring into nothingness as though he had forgotten what he had just then been thinking. By the time these episodes were wearing off, he found himself missing periods of time, the time changing from nine a.m. To ten thirty without him being able to recall what had happened or where that time had gone.

This caused him grave concern, as this was time he should have been spending in lectures, in studying and doing all the things he had come to university to do in the first place, namely, to improve his chances of future success in the workplace, in whatever avenue he chose to pursue. Already these were being jeopardised.

He put these absences down to side effects of the benzodiazepines. He had read that this was a potential issue with them, and he didn't need to do a great deal of convincing himself in order to stop using them, replacing them with the F and H. He much preferred the feelings that they gave him anyway, although he had found that he had stabilised, for want of a better expression, whilst on them, he overcame that by increasing his does to one and a half tablets, which kept him where he wanted to be.

No longer was he on a trajectory of ever-increasing elation, riding the highs like Sancho Panza on the bed cloth; now, he transformed from focused, to happy, to elated, but not to euphoric. If only he could manage the downside of the slope. The purgatorial side of the butterfly. The dark days of depression, dejection and never-ending time.

He tried to stay positive, as much as he could, recalling those feelings of pure happiness while the drug was still at play in his system. He imagined it like a miniscule feather, floating around his system, gently tickling his delicate nerve endings, making him giggle like an innocent baby. The laughter spreading infectiously, as though by some strange spell, in the same way a babies laugh spreads contagiously around a room, lighting up the soul of all who are fortunate enough to be graced by it. So, the drug spread around his system, lighting up his soul, allowing him to forget the cataclysmic dilemma he was really in.

It was about the only solace he had left now, and he needed to make sure he could continue with that solace for as long as was necessary. The alternative would be a lifetime of problems of nightmarish proportions, being unable to differentiate between the real world and the living incarnation of his own dreams.

He knew he'd have some dreams that were good, and stayed good, but he was fearful that even the dreams that were, on the surface, good, would metamorphosize into some horrific nerve-wrenching problem that would also leave him highly stressed, or worse. For example, how long would it be before he had the dream of falling? He had had that a few times, always waking up - often with a start - just before he landed. But how would that map out in the real world? would he just stop a few feet off the ground and have to somehow step back onto terra firma? would he magically just appear somewhere else, completely disconnected, as usually happened in dreams? or would he fall and land with a painful thud? Would his own dreams actually hurt him and put him in hospital even?

These thoughts occupied his mind constantly, over the next few weeks, but, each time, his thoughts circled back to the same dominating thought. That was, that he needed more of the amphetamines.

Or maybe something stronger?

The idea of needing something a little more potent came to him as an unexpected revelation, towards the tail end of the third week, or maybe it was the fourth? He had no real concept of time any longer. He was down to his last half a dozen tablets, and, staring at the little plastic bag whilst riding another roller coaster of misery and depression that concatenated itself onto the end of the previous high, like night following day, he began contemplating events.

He had not dreamed for three weeks, or maybe four, now, which was the thin silver lining to the otherwise cumulonimbus sized grey cloud that he felt was darkening his horizons at the moment. He had not dreamed because he had not actually slept properly for the duration of those days. The benzodiazepines had left him feeling strange. He didn't so much feel as though he had slept, more like he had blinked, very slowly, and by the time his eyes had reopened several hours had passed and he felt a bit fresher and less fatigued.

When he had felt an ominous sense of Deja-vu whilst shopping in the supermarket, he decided there and then to stop taking them. It wasn't a difficult decision for him to make, he had already been toying with the idea of sticking to the F and H anyway, and this feeling that the sleeping pills were not doing quite the job he had hoped they would, was literally the only push he needed to make the leap.

This led him to his next issue. As he stared at the bag, it occurred to him that he needed a refill. He'd been taking two pills at a time for the last few days now, and only had three days' worth left. He needed to get hold of Josh again, which meant he needed to leave the apartment.

At some point, he had rationalised, or irrationalised, that if he stayed inside his apartment, then the chances of anything bad happening - in the faint chance that he might somehow fall asleep and begin dreaming - would be limited due to his environment being likewise limited.

He didn't think he had been out of the apartment in a while, although his sleep deprived mind was struggling to calculate exactly how long it had really been.

Not sleeping had left the days blurring into one insanity inducing stain of meaningless time, separated only by intervals of darkness from outside the windows that, sometimes felt like the planet was blinking, and other times like the light was so enamoured by his presence that it would never leave him.

He vaguely recalled noticing, at some time, that his cupboards were nearly empty, and he had ventured to the local corner shop to get some supplies, but he also had a hazy memory of not being hungry so only purchasing a few bars of chocolate.

There was also a foggy memory of the girls visiting a couple of times, and that the three of them had gotten into a ferocious argument. But that seemed as though it happened forever ago, if it even did happen. He couldn't solidify the memory into anything coherent. They had left in a temper; or had they? did they storm out? or had he thrown them out. It was all so hazy. Maybe he had unknowingly fallen asleep briefly and dreamed it, hence it being so elusive to him. He would have to try keep it to the front of his mind in case he noticed any signs of that happening.

Regardless of that, he needed more pills, or powder, he wasn't bothered, which meant he needed to go find Josh and whilst he was out, he would pick up a few more bars of chocolate as the thought of them was giving him a hunger.

* * * *

He spent the next few days scouring the University buildings in search of Josh, but he couldn't see hide nor hair of him anywhere.

By now, his friends, other students and members of the University staff were noticing Jonathan's increasingly erratic mannerisms and nervous behaviour. He kept asking people if they had seen Josh, but no-one admitted to even knowing who Josh was. Paranoia began to set in, he felt a conspiracy was being enacted against him again, the more people he asked, the more the paranoia grew until it reached almost Brobdingnagian proportions. The only people he had told of his intention to use drugs had been Elizabeth and Jennifer, and both had been against the idea as a course of action.

The only way then, he figured, that everyone would be denying knowledge of Josh would be if the girls were now conspiring against him, trying to prevent him from obtaining more drugs. Which meant that he could no longer trust them.

What could he do? he needed more drugs, he needed more money with which to buy them, and he also needed to find Josh who he could buy them from. These became the only things he thought about, and he sat brooding over the matter for some time.

Eventually, he had convinced himself that the girls knew where Josh was, and that they were purposefully doing whatever they could to keep him away from him. He was also certain that they were colluding with the rest of the students to block his every chance of finding him, which meant he couldn't trust any of the other students either. He had to confront the girls directly, and force them to tell him where Josh was. He would beat it out of them if he really had to.

Chapter XV

Elizabeth could hear a distant drum banging, but she could not discern from where it came. Louder and louder, clearer and clearer it got, until she crashed back into consciousness.

Someone was banging on the apartment door.

Groggily she turned to look at the clock, it was nearly four a.m.

"What the hell!?" she said to herself, and climbed out of bed to go see who was disturbing her at this ungodly hour, and give them a sound piece of her mind. It was probably some drunk students at the wrong apartment, she thought, and by God are they going to regret doing so.

She opened the door to see a rather wild looking Jonathan standing before her. It took her a little by surprise as they hadn't really seen him in a few weeks. He looked terrible, his eyes were bloodshot and grey ringed, the hair on his head had been left to grow out and the patchiness resembled an overused tennis ball. His face was gaunt and almost skeletal.

He looked like death, but an angry death, an unbridled rage pulsating from him in waves.

"Where is he? eh? where've you hidden him!?" Jonathan growled at her, through gritted teeth, pushing his way into the apartment.

"What the hell, Jonathan!" she asked, both confused and angry at him for barging in like that. He was looking around the apartment for something, his gaze darting from one place to the next, like a predatory searching out a hidden prey. He looked desperate to find something.

"What are you talking about? hidden who? and what the hell kind of time do you call this? it's four a.m. For God's sake!"

"You know exactly what I'm talking about!" he turned, directing his anger and accusatory gaze directly at her.

By this point, Jennifer, who could normally sleep through just about anything, had been woken by the furore, and had come out of her room to see what the fracas was about. She had moved in with Elizabeth after her first-year halls of residency had come to an end, and who better for her to move in with than a friend, who also happened to be in the same classes.

"Where is he? Where's Josh?" he continued, his gaze now flicking between the two of them. Elizabeth looked at Jennifer, confused, hoping she knew what Jonathan was talking about, but seeing an equally confused look on Jennifers face, turned back to Jonathan.

"Josh? who's Josh?" she asked.

"Don't give me that!" he growled, "you know exactly who he is. The guy I bought the gear from. You're the only two who knew what I was doing, and you both disapproved. I can't believe you'd betray me like this! I need to find him; I need to get more. I can't risk dreaming again, you know I can't!"

Jennifer and Elizabeth looked at each other, confounded. A whole conversation flowed between them, like electricity flowing down wires, unseen. Yes, Jonathan had told them of his plans to use drugs temporarily to solve his problem, and yes, they had been averse to the idea, but they did not know who Josh was and they could also see that Jonathan was clearly not in his right mind now. Erratic, volatile and carrying an anger they had never seen in him before. They needed to try calm him down so they could talk and try get some sense out of him.

"Jonathan," said Elizabeth, as calmly as she could "we have no idea who you're talking about. We've never met anyone called Josh..."

"Don't lie!" he screamed at her, cutting her off "you know exactly who he is. The guy I bought the stuff from. You just want to stop me from seeing him so I can't get any more."

Elizabeth looked at him, shocked into silence at the aggression he was directing at her. She really had no idea what he was talking about, they didn't even know that he had bought any yet.

"You-you-you bought drugs!?..." she stammered. But his patience had run out, he lunged for her, grabbing her by the throat.

"Where is he!!?" He was apoplectic with rage, veins bulging in his neck and forehead, spittle spraying as he yelled into her face.

"Jonathan! Stop it!!" Jennifer screamed, desperately, from behind him. All his focus had been on Elizabeth stood in front of him and he had forgotten Jennifer was there for a moment, the sound of her voice distracted him, and he turned his head to look at her.

She was holding something in her hands, pointing it straight at him. He let go of Elizabeth's throat and she dropped to the floor gasping for breath.

Jonathan turned his attention to Jennifer. She was staring straight at him, defiantly, trying to look as fearless and confident as she could muster.

"She's telling the truth." She said firmly. "Now you need to leave, before you do something you might regret."

Jonathan looked straight at her, directly into her eyes. His gaze burrowing deep into her soul, searching for the truth, looking for any hint that what she was saying was a lie. He moved his gaze from her to through her. He felt unnervingly calm - considering the rage and hate he felt towards these two so called friends. He was a predator that had cornered its prey, knowing it was cornered and that it was just a matter of when it wanted to pounce and put it out of its misery. He had that calm confidence of knowing the inevitable.

He gave a wry smile of satisfaction as he took a step towards her and saw her take a nervous step back.

Jennifer looked straight into Jonathan's bloodshot eyes, he was past the point of rationality, or of being reasoned with. He looked almost feral, so she didn't hesitate. The only thing she'd had to hand was a small canister of deodorant, which is what she had picked up and pointed at him. Clearly, he didn't view it as any kind of threat. She pressed the nozzle and sprayed it straight into his face.

Jonathan's senses were hit with multiple sensations simultaneously. The coldness of the spray, the wetness of it, the perfume in his nose, the burning in his eyes and the choking of his lungs all battled for dominance and overwhelmed him. The attacks to his olfactory system and his breathing winning out. His instinct of survival, however, managed to overwhelm any prior idea that he might have had of harming others disappearing as he dropped to his knees coughing and gasping for breath. His eyes and nose streaming with tears and snot as his bodies defence mechanism kicked in to try remove the irritant from his nasal passage and eyeballs. He expectorated heavily in order to try remove as much of it as he could from his lungs and throat, all without success. In and amongst this sensational overload, he could hear someone screaming.

"Now get out!... GET OUT!"

He was so disorientated that he couldn't tell where the sound was coming from, but a voice deep inside him was agreeing with the sentiment 'yes, get out. Don't leave yourself open to attack. You're in no fit state to defend yourself' it said.

He tried to blink away the tears, so that he might see which way to exit, but they wouldn't disappear long enough, they were just replaced by fresh tears streaming from his eyes causing everything to be blurred and indecipherable.

He reached out his hand to grab hold of the door, firstly as a known exit, but also for stability; with no real visual ability and his nose and lungs still burning, it made him very unstable and disorientated, and therefore unable to move anywhere. It took all his concentration to avoid falling back onto his hands and knees, although he considered that crawling might be a viable way to navigate himself out of harm's way. He waved his hand around some more, and felt it bang against something. He grabbed it, the thickness told him that it was the door, and he reached out his other hand to meet it, then used them to guide himself out of the doorway into the hallway beyond.

Despite desperately wanting to get out, the pain in his eyes was angering him beyond rationality. How dare they!

A voice in the back of his mind was goading him to get some revenge before he finally left. He reached an arm behind him and grabbed hold of whoever it was. He couldn't see well enough to tell, but he grabbed hold of her, managing to catch her by the throat and spun around so he could try push her back against the door. No sooner had he turned than he felt a pain in his groin; it welled up to his stomach immediately. He thought he was going to be sick. She had kneed him in the privates and that was more than enough to finish him off. He bent double, rotated back around and felt another kick on his backside that sent him tumbling out of the door.

He heard the door slam shut behind him and the locks being set as he curled up in a ball, one hand holding his groin, the other trying to clean the burning sensation from his eyes.

He sat outside the doorway, propped up against the wall, and caught his breath as he kept trying to stop the streaming of his eyes and nose. Once he had some visibility back, he slowly got up and made his way back to his own apartment. He was intensely disappointed. This had not gone how he had planned it.

* * * *

Finally back at this apartment, he sat in a realisation of defeat. He was out of drugs; he couldn't find Josh and he had failed in getting the girls to tell him where he was.

A dark mood spread over him, enveloping him as he resigned himself to the fact that he was now entirely at the mercy of whatever dreams his mind could conjure up when he finally succumbed to sleep. And, given how much these recent events had bothered him, it meant he could be in for a really bad time of things.

The tears that now fell were not the result of the perfume, but a result of an abject sorrow and the futility that he was powerless to stop any of it now. He wished he had bought more drugs when he'd had the chance. But, even had he the foresight to know, he doubted he would have been able to afford the amount he would have needed. "Oh, how I wish I were rich" he muttered to himself through the tears.

Chapter XVI

Jonathan slowly opened his reddened eyes. It was broad daylight.

He looked around his room in an attempt to try reorientate himself. He didn't remember much from the time he got back from Elizabeth and Jennifers apartment to the point he fell asleep. He presumed he had fallen asleep. He remembered getting in, washing his face and swilling his mouth out with water to get rid of as much of the perfume as he could. He was livid at Jennifer for spraying him in the face like that, he was only asking where Josh was. But then his hazy memory began to fill in some of the pieces of the jigsaw that composed the scene, and, though he was still mad at her, he did kind of understand.

That being said, if it weren't for the fact that they were keeping Josh away from him, then he wouldn't have needed to get like that with them to begin with, so it was all their own fault.

Once he could find Josh, he would be able to get himself level again and then he could start to think about how to rebuild bridges with them.

"Ohh!" he groaned, his head thick and heavy as he remembered more details of the night. He had roamed the streets, half blind and in a rage, searching for Josh. All to no avail, and now he was realising what that meant for him.

He wasn't sure why he had thought Josh would be out at that time of night, or morning, but he was so desperate for a refill that his mind had convinced him the would be lucky, after all, his previous encounters with Josh had all been equally random.

He looked around his room to see what time it was. The clock was telling him it was five past twelve. That couldn't be right. It would mean he had only slept for about six hours; but his body did not feel tired enough to have only slept that long, especially after going so many weeks without sleep now.

He lay back on the bed, trying to decide how he thought he should feel.

If he normally slept longer than around nine hours, he would find he would awaken with a headache from dehydration, and if not an actual headache, he would feel very heavy headed. Likewise, if he didn't sleep long enough, his body would let him know. The fatigue in his muscles, general lethargy and constant yawning were all the usual signs that he had had insufficient sleep, but he felt none of these. What he did feel, or rather notice, was that he was struggling to formulate any memories. He knew that he was angry at Elizabeth and Jennifer, and that they had had quite the altercation about Josh's disappearance. He had also been sprayed in the face with some kind of aerosol, perfume or deodorant, but he was no longer feeling any effects - which he was grateful for. All in all, he was generally feeling as though he had lost time, about six hours' worth, to be precise.

A moment later he began to smile, a big beaming smile. Lost time meant dreamless sleep. He felt a weight lift from him that he didn't even realise he was carrying.

He sat up and immediately noticed he had changed clothes. He didn't remember doing that. He'd been wearing Jeans and a T-shirt before, but now had a shirt and trousers on, which perplexed him a little.

He focused on when he might have changed, but nothing came to mind. Had he showered to try remove more of the aerosol from him?

He shook his head deciding not to think about it any further, it would come to him in due course.

His stomach rumbled, reminding him that he hadn't eaten in almost a full day, so he made his way to the kitchen to find something. The cupboards were empty with the exception of a single bar of chocolate. As was the fridge. He couldn't remember running out of food, but then he couldn't remember buying any food lately either. In the back of his mind, the faintest of voices tried to whisper something to him, but it was too quiet, inaudible.

He closed the fridge, grabbed his wallet and set off out of the apartment.

On opening the apartment door, the first thing he noticed was wooden decking beneath his feet, which caught him off guard. When had they redecorated? and why with decking?

As his eyes moved upwards, he could see the decking led to wooden steps that led down into a lush green meadow, grass, roughly eight inches tall swished and swayed in a breeze he could not feel.

He stood, rooted to the spot in confusion. His brain at odds with his eyes, the latter telling him quite conclusively what he could see before him, the former adamantly refusing to accept it.

In order to attempt to further convince his brain, his eyes followed the meadow off into the distance which led him to a large lake, several hundred meters away, the waters a cool looking fresh cyan in colour. Crystal clear, reflecting the orange and yellow of sun-drenched clouds from the sky above. At the farthest end of the lake, the clear turquoise waters darkened and merged into the lush greenery of trees that were on the far shore, those same tree's growing up the side of a huge mountain range. There had to have been tens of thousands of trees. The vivid greenery of the trees themselves merged into greyish-green and deep blue colours of the mountainside, the blue appearing to come, somehow, from the sky above. Everything appeared to meld into each other seamlessly, as one glorious and unified image. The moss, shale, ferns and stones inseparable from one another, a harmony of nature. It was breathtaking.

He let his eyes scan the vista before him.

The clouds in the sky a golden orange, both absorbing and filtering the hue of light from the bright orb of the sun; the rest of the sky a gloriously fresh pale blue, barely a blemish in the sky, only interrupted occasionally by the odd clean looking wispy cloud, like candy floss floating on by. The crispness of it all gave the impression of being cold, yet he felt nothing; it was like he was stood in some kind of invisible, climate-controlled bubble. The scenery reminding him of a picture-perfect postcard from some European country, Austria or Switzerland, or somewhere similar to that. The sheer beauty of it all mesmerised him. Any, and all problems that he might have had, were they not already forgotten due to the bizzarity of the whole situation, were now completely gone.

His gaze made the return journey back down the mountainside, across the lake and back to the meadow. In the furthest corner of which, he could see, stood entirely in isolation, what appeared to be a brown cow, casually chewing at the fresh green grass.

He wasn't sure if it was his imagination, but he felt as though it was returning his own inquisitive gaze. After a few seconds, the cow, for he could see now that it definitely was a cow, paused its task of chewing and raised its head slightly, as though to give him its full attention.

A shiver ran down Jonathan's spine, the fixed empty gaze from the animal unnerving him for a reason he couldn't explain, but he felt as though the cow was trying to communicate with him telepathically. Did it know he couldn't understand it?

He tried to telepathically return that sentiment back to it.

Every few seconds it took another slow chew, eyeing him distantly. The more he looked, the more he was certain it was trying to communicate with him in some fashion. But he was still unable to understand, so he just returned the cow's gaze.

The longer he looked at it, the more the sense of disapproval grew in his gut. He didn't know where this feeling came from, or why the cow was so disapproving of him looking at it, but, as the seconds ticked away, the more that seed grew inside him.

He now imagined he could see a change in the facial expression of the animal, from a docile placidity to a more menacing look now, as though he was somehow angering it.

As if to reiterate the point, it took a step closer to him, and paused, assessing to see if the foe had been unnerved.

Jonathan stayed exactly where he was, he felt an unusual level of intrigue into the animal's behaviour, and he kept watching to see what it did next.

It took another step closer, and, again, paused to assess.

Jonathan, in spite of the increasingly unnerving nature of the advance, was fascinated by this display and wondered what it meant.

She kept her eyes fixed, rigidly, on the strange animal. It was about two hundred yards away and she suspected it could not see her. If she moved carefully enough, she thought she may be able to get close enough, but she had to move slowly so as not to frighten it away.

It hadn't moved at all in the last thirty seconds or so, and she had managed to get a few paces closer. She took another smooth, careful step forward and waited. Still, it didn't move.

Things were looking promising. She took another careful step forwards and paused again.

Then another ... And another.

Jonathan kept his gaze fixed on the animal's strange behaviour. He'd never seen anything like it, the cow took a careful step closer, then paused and stayed still as it kept its eyes fixed on him. He felt no fear, he had no need, it was only a cow; and while he didn't think it would be frightened of him, he didn't want to make any sudden movements and risk startling it.

He watched it creep another step forward. It kept creeping forward in this fashion, one step at a time until it was maybe forty meters away, where it stopped, dead still, and stared at him, fixedly, for a whole minute or more. Jonathan was transfixed.

Suddenly, it moved rapidly, morphing into a full-grown tiger, leaping towards him, roaring. No longer a docile harmless cow but a life-threatening predator. His heart leapt up into his mouth, the transformation from cow to tiger coming in the blink of an eye. Panic overwhelming him as he turned, frantically scrambling his way back up the stairs towards the log cabin, tripping over the top step, sprawling onto the decking; but he had no time to delay, he couldn't stall, he could hear the tiger bounding towards him, its large paws clawing the earth underneath as it gripped for purchase to propel itself towards its prey.

For a reason that he could not, nor ever would be able to, explain, he glanced back to see exactly where it was. As his hand gripped the door handle pulling it open, he regretted the fraction of a second that he had wasted in looking, certain he had just condemned himself to an agonizing death. It was only a few meters behind and preparing to pounce.

Time seemed to slow to an almost stop. He darted into the doorway and was pulling the door shut as he saw the underbelly of the tiger stretch out above him.

He dived into the cabin, the door slamming behind him, but instead of hitting the hard cabin floor, he just fell. The last thing he heard was the thud of the tiger colliding with the door as he fell down a deep hole.

Either time was still proceeding at an exceptionally protracted rate, or he was falling a long way.

After what felt like several minutes - but, in all reality, was actually more like twenty seconds, he noticed what appeared to be wire cables and steel caging whizzing past. He blinked, slowly, and when his eyes opened, he felt a pressure against his cheek, and became aware that his face was pressed against a floor. The flooring was around two meters by two meters, and he let his eyes move around the space before he pushed himself up to a crouch, before finally standing.

He was stood inside what was apparently an elevator, and it looked to be descending.

After a moment, it stopped as the light on the panel showed it had reached the ground floor and the doors swished open.

He stepped out and took a look around. He was in a large, bright, shopping mall, three stories high. Shops of all kinds lined either side of each level. Bright neon lights advertising their brand, inviting any willing shopper to enter and spend their hard-earned money on products they likely didn't even really need.

There was a large glass ceiling high above, covering the vast cathedral like complex, offering a comforting silica-based umbrella of safety against the elements to all who wandered beneath it.

He looked down the floor he was on, it seemed to go on forever. A large water fountain, about thirty meters in front of him, spouted jets of spume that made an incredibly artistic water feature. Beyond that, a huge fir tree, decorated with silver tinsel, and small white lights glittering in a sparkling winter scene. Maybe it was Christmas here?

He looked around at all the shops, there seemed to be a shop for everything; cookie shops, phone shops, shoes, clothes, TV's, adult underwear, toys, carpets, books, you name it, there was a shop for it here. He doubted there was anything you could not buy in this mall.

People walked up and down the concourse, entering and leaving shops, seemingly randomly, and, also seemingly oblivious to the presence of anyone else. A background rumble of the myriad conversations happening all melding into one indistinguishable sound.

Jonathan didn't know what to do, nor did he know where to go. He didn't really know where he was aside from the inside of a shopping mall of some kind. What he did have, was a strange tingling sensation, in the back of his mind, that he was being watched.

He let his eyes continue to scan the area in front of him, the hair on the back of his neck standing on end, and a tingle running down his spine, as though someone had, ever so faintly, run the tip of their finger down his neck. He shivered. The feeling of being watched grew, and was now coming from many different places. Was he just being paranoid? He didn't think so, he had no real need to be, but still, his eyes searched frantically to seek out whoever was watching.

He turned around, expecting to see the elevator at his back, but the mall stretched out behind him in the same way it did in front, a mirror image.

Then he saw them.

Hiding behind the fir tree, a man with a shiny black beard and dressed all in black, peered out. Jonathan probably wouldn't have noticed him if he hadn't abruptly darted back behind the tree, trying not to be seen. Then he saw someone else, also dressed in black, also with a black beard, in a shop entrance to the right of him, also trying to stay out of view.

Now he knew how they were dressed he looked around further, scanning the mall to see how many of them there were. He saw one on the right-hand balcony, another on the left-hand balcony. All peering at him creepily.

They were all dressed the same, all in black, all with black beards. They could be each other's doppelganger, and, though he had no idea who they were, he had an overwhelming inclination to flee. Something told him he had to avoid them getting hold of him.

So, he turned and ran.

Except, no matter how fast he tried to run, he didn't seem to move anywhere. It was like he was in a wind tunnel, no matter how much effort he put in, some invisible, unfelt, force-field held him back. He could see the floor beneath him moving under his feet, but everything else stayed where it was, like running on a treadmill, the matting goes away underneath you, but the same four walls are around you. Fixed, immoveable constants.

He looked around to see where the figures in black were now. They had sprung into action and had set off running after him, the two on the ground floor, behind him, now brandishing what looked like batons, or worse still, machetes.

No-one else in the mall paid the slightest attention to them. It was as though they didn't even see them, like they didn't exist to anyone other than Jonathan.

Via some mystical portent, he was now moving. Running at the speed that he had originally intended to move, and he narrowly avoided tripping over the low wall that bordered the fir tree which he had now arrived at, hurdling over its corner at the very last second in order to avoid breaking his shin.

He couldn't avoid having to slow down though, but still he carried on. He was fast coming up to an escalator, and he quickly assessed where the doppelgangers were in relation to him. He had two choices, up the escalator or go further along the concourse, and he had mere seconds in which to choose.

He flicked his gaze into the distance. It never seemed to end, the same landmarks repeated on to infinity. Beyond the escalator was another water feature, about twenty meters further along. Twenty meters beyond that, another fir tree, which, superficially at least, seemed to be identical to the one he had just nearly tripped over. Beyond that, yet another escalator.

He looked again at the escalator that was now upon him. He didn't think he would have enough speed to get up the escalator to the first floor before one of the doppelgangers got there, and he strongly suspected he would not be able to fight them off. So, he quickly swerved to the right of the escalator entrance, manoeuvred around the back of it, which temporarily blocked his visibility from the men who were following.

He knew he wouldn't be able to sustain this pace of running for much longer - he was amazed he had been able to keep it up for so long already - and he darted his gaze around for a safe haven that he could run to and take refuge.

As if on command, he saw an entranceway to a children's toy shop which had a signpost inviting him in.

This doorway looked like the stereotypical 'Toy Store' he recalled seeing in many an old Christmas movie. Toy houses in the window, green holly and red and white candy canes hanging everywhere.

It seemed too fortuitous to be ignored, so he accepted the invitation and darted inside.

Once inside, he made his way deeper into the store, manoeuvring around displays in order to try blend in with the crowd of shoppers already perusing the items on offer.

He was amazed at the size of the place, it was huge. He gazed around, taking in the whole amazing display. It was a vast warehouse of entertainment, all of which was directed towards providing young children with every conceivable toy to keep them entertained and happy.

There was a strange aura to the place as well. In spite of the size of it, and the accompanying bustle from the crowds dispersed amongst its many rows and aisles, there was a palpable serenity to it all. Children stood, transfixed by the toys they held. Smiles of wonderment on their faces, some looking up to adoring parents, silently appealing to have the toy purchased for them, others beaming with joy because their parents had just agreed to gift them the toy. Jonathan could not see a single unhappy child, none upset that their appeals had been declined. It was as though they were under some kind of a spell.

He listened harder for any kind of what he would consider a normal sound of a dejected, upset child, but this store seemed eerily unique in that regard. All background noises were of toys clacking, tinkling, whirring or grinding, mixed with giggles of joy.

In the furthest corner of the shop, he could see a giant, plastic, motorised Santa Claus, arm waving, 'ho-ho-ho'ing' merrily away. Big nose, red cheeks either side of a beaming smile welcomed one and all.

Jonathan started to walk towards him, as calm as he had ever been. The people in black, who just moments ago had been chasing him - possibly to kill him - now not even a memory.

He arrived at the staircase that led to Santa's platform, reached out to take hold of the banister and pulled a car door open, climbing into the passenger seat.

Santa Claus sat in the driver's seat, one hand on the steering wheel, looking across at him, waiting for him to close the door and fasten his seatbelt.

The big friendly grin on his face evincing the fact that he had not a care in the world. Jonathan closed the door, slot the seatbelt into place and Santa set off driving.

Jonathan sat quietly, staring out of the window, as though this was always the plan.

A sprawling barren desert spread out into the distance; only the occasional Joshua Tree and cacti broke up the scene, with the exception of tumbleweed.

The bizzarity of everything that was happening never seemed to be of any concern to Jonathan. At no point did his mind ask why he was jumping from place to place, scene to scene, it just seemed to go along with it and focus on that present moment. If only he could be this indifferent the rest of the time.

Now, he just sat quietly and thought of nothing.

"Santa." he said after a moment, looking back across at the jovial character sitting in the driving seat. " Is this a dream?"

"Ho-ho-ho!"

"...or is this the re-enactment of a dream I've had, that has now come to life?"

"Ho-ho-ho!"

"...and how am I supposed to tell?"

"Ho-ho-ho!"

"How do I know if I am dreaming or awake anymore?"

Santa dropped his smile, fixed his gaze, solemnly on Jonathan.

"Does it matter?"

"Of course it matters."

"Why?" came Santa's earnest reply. Jonathan was a little caught off guard for a moment. He thought about it, but he couldn't fathom what Santa was getting at.

"What do you mean?" he asked.

"Well. Whether you're dreaming or whether your dream has manifested into reality, you cannot control either. They are either just a figment of your imagination or a representation of it. It's not your actual life. It's just a distraction, a distraction from your actual life and what you *can* do, what you have control over. So, what does it matter if it's just that you are dreaming it or that it's a representation of that same dream?"

Jonathan returned his gaze back out to the desert and thought this over.

"It doesn't matter?" he said to himself, half questioningly.

"No. They are not real, they are pipe dreams, none of them are permanent, just brief echoes of what could be, and as a result, you have cast aside your real dreams, your aspirations, chasing these. While you do so, you are destined to live in perpetual torment."

Jonathan sat, forlorn and miserable at what he had just heard. He tried to think of something else to say, but his mind was blank again, like he was drifting away.

He felt dejected, resigning himself to his fate. He opened the car door and swung his legs out and sat, perched on the edge of his bed. He looked around to see what this new scene was.

He was back in his apartment.

The phone rang on the bedside table. He reached across, picked it up and answered.

"Did you dream you could fly?" came Elizabeth's voice, tentatively, from the headset.

"No." he replied and hung up. He was too preoccupied to be going over trivialities like that, so he sat, thinking. Thinking through the conversation he'd just had with Santa Claus; he needed to figure it out.

'Am I still dreaming?' he asked himself, 'or am I awake and this is a real version of the dream? or am I really in reality and there's no more dream? and it's done with till the next one? ... How do I know? surely there's a way for me to know the difference? this room looks real enough, this is my bedroom, my apartment. Maybe I'm not dreaming anymore? ... Was I dreaming just now? it felt real... Maybe... Okay, it was too weird to be real-real, but how do I know whether it was dream or dream-real? If my dreams become real, what are the limits of the possibilities?... How am I ever to know the difference between dream-real and actual reality?'

He sat, with his head in his hands despairing at the situation, weeping. It was all too much.

'How do I make this all stop?' he wept to himself. 'I don't know what to do. I don't know how to cope. Who can help me? I'm all alone in this Hell, with no way out, and his gentle weeping built to full blow crying as the panic and desperation crescendoed, like an avalanche pounding inside his mind.

"I wish I was dead!" he cried.

After he had cried himself dry, his comment about being dead resurfaced in his thoughts, pulsing, like a lighthouse beacon, warning where land was.

'Thats the answer' he thought. 'You can't die in your dreams, which must mean that I can't die in dream-reality either. That's how I could tell.' He looked around for something to use to test the hypothesis. The long extension from the lamp would be ideal. It was over two meters long, so would be perfect. If this was a dream, or dream-real, then at some point it would stop him, he guessed by switching scenes to somewhere, or something, else.

It was perfect.

He tied a noose at one end, stood on a chair and wrapped the plug end round the iron lightshade that hung from the ceiling.

There was very little give in the chord and when he kicked the chair from beneath his feet he hung, six to eight inches from the floor. Panic surged through him immediately, adrenaline pumping. His feet kicking around as the plastic chord dug into his neck, stopping the blood flow both too and from his brain. He was choking, the fear rose rapidly, he had no way out of this, and he struggled violently to try free himself, somehow.

Anyhow.

Stars exploded in his eyes like an uncontrollable firework display. But, after a short time struggling, darkness settled over his vision as he lost consciousness, and he hung there limply.

A few minutes later he was dead.

He wasn't dreaming.

Chapter XVII

It was a mild day, the day of Jonathan's funeral. Clear blue skies, full of birdsong and newly sprouting flowers, contradicted the dark, morose, mood that had settled over both Jennifer and Elizabeth's spirits.

Inside their hearts, the clouds were black and grim, and heavy torrential rains fell that mirrored the tears that had fallen from their eyes.

Jennifer looked around at the people who were gathered. It was a small group, only a couple of dozen, maybe less, and none of them were of her own age.

No-one else from the University, aside from Elizabeth, were in attendance. Her heart had fallen even further at that realisation; and the feeling of sorrow was temporarily replaced by an anger. An anger at the injustice of Jonathan being dead. An anger at her university colleagues caring so little, and an anger at them not even bothering to pay their respects.

She glanced over at Elizabeth. Above all, she resented *her*.

Jennifer was interrupted from her thoughts by a feint bustle of activity amongst the other mourners. She could see that they were looking off into the distance, off to her left. She followed their gaze and saw the hearse slowly making its way into the cemetery gates.

A tear slowly formed and ran down her cheek as the realisation set in that she was now bearing witness to Jonathan's final journey.

She tried her best to supress an outburst of tears, but all that did was cause them to come out in coughs and snivels.

Retrieving a handkerchief from her purse, she began to wipe her eyes, grateful for the black veil she wore that she could hide behind and conceal the redness of her eyes, and the mascara that she felt sure must be running down her face already.

She tidied herself up as best she could, and her mind began to drift back to that fateful afternoon.

It was Elizabeth who had found Jonathan's body, a few days later, when she had gone round to see him to try get an apology from him for the way that he had behaved towards them the last time they had spoken.

This had triggered the first seeds of resentment between them, and it budded and grew rapidly afterwards.

They had both been on the receiving end of Jonathan's anger that day, and Jennifer felt that she had as much right to be involved in getting an apology as Elizabeth had. Yet Elizabeth had, purposefully as far as she was concerned, kept her out of it.

It seemed that Elizabeth had text Jonathan several times, trying to extend an olive branch, so she claimed, and when those texts had garnered no response, she had then tried to phone him. Why had Elizabeth not contacted her too? That's what Jennifer wanted to know. Why hadn't she involved her then? They were the questions Elizabeth refused to even acknowledge, let alone answer.

After the third unanswered call, so her story went, she had gotten worried and instead of getting in touch with her so they could go together, she had once again excluded her, and gone round to see him on her own.

To Jennifer, Elizabeth had acted as though *she* didn't matter, like she didn't even exist, and *her* feelings were completely irrelevant. The more she thought about it, the more her resentment grew, until it was a seething knot built up inside her stomach.

She distracted her eyes from the hearse back to where Elizabeth was standing. She too had tears rolling down her face.

* * * *

Elizabeth had never felt so alone in all her life. The image of Jonathan hanging from the ceiling, and the smell of *that* room, had given her non-stop nightmares ever since. They plagued her every thought, everywhere she went she was reminded, she couldn't scrub it from her mind. She was falling apart, and what was worse, she had no-one she felt she could talk to about it. No one who could help her deal with it.

The feeling of utter helplessness suffocated her. Not only did she not know how to help herself, but it was compounded by the fact that she hadn't been able to help Jonathan either.

They had known Jonathan was living the torment of his dreams coming true. They had gotten past the naive, optimistic, idea that having your dreams come true was a great thing, quite quickly. These were not dreams, they were nightmares, just as that creepy man in the bookshop had said. Even the dreams they thought would only result in good, had turned sour due to overlooked twists of fate.

For all she knew, Jonathan was in the grips of one of these dreams gone wrong the day he had hung himself.

She clung to that idea for all she was worth. The thought of Jonathan voluntarily committing suicide was too much for her to bear.

If only she had been more understanding. Had she been, then she felt she wouldn't have had that argument. They could have listened to him, heard him out, tried to understand better whatever dream he was trying to navigate at the time. Helped him get through it.

Hindsight was the devil that was sent to torment her all the more.

She thought about what else she might have been able to do.

She had text him **CAN WE TALK?**

Maybe that was a mistake? Maybe she shouldn't have text him at all? No, she should have gone straight round to his apartment, talked to him face to face.

But he would still have been dead, that wouldn't have changed, she would merely have found his body earlier. No, the only way she could have stopped this would be to have not had the argument in the first place. But he *was* hysterical, and they had no idea what he was talking about. How could she have avoided it?

Her head hurt trying to think about it. She couldn't think of any way she could have avoided seeing what she saw.

The thoughts of finding the body brought her mind back to it, no matter how much she wanted to avoid thinking about it.

She had been texting him every half hour. With each text both her anxiety and worry had built. After the fourth one she had abandoned texting and rang him instead, thinking that maybe he had just misplaced his phone somewhere and simply not heard it ping when her text came in. Maybe she would help him find his phone by ringing, he'd be able to hear where it rang from and locate it once again.

She had visions of him sat wondering where he might have lost it and then being relieved to hear it ringing.

But the calls hadn't been answered either. This had worried her even more. She knew they had quarrelled, and that words, harsh words, had been exchanged. Jennifer had even sprayed him with her deodorant to avoid him attacking them. Even so, she felt that after a few days to calm down, Jonathan would at least talk to her. They were best friends and, as bad as the situation had been, it wasn't insurmountable. Heck, she had already been willing to talk it through with him, try to put it behind them, and she was sure Jonathan was more forgiving than she was.

After her third attempted call had gone unanswered, her concern about him had peaked and she went round to see him.

She had spent a full ten minutes knocking, with no answer, before trying some of the neighbours' doors to see if any of them had seen anything of him recently.

They all said more or less the same thing, that they hadn't seen him. From what they said, or more precisely, what they didn't say, it seemed no one on the floor paid a great deal of notice of anyone else. A couple of them weren't aware anyone even lived in that apartment.

Getting no joy from the neighbours, she went around some of their usual haunts. There weren't too many places they went to hang out, a mere handful, but the most popular one by far was the coffee shop, which is where she started.

He hadn't been there, and the barista hadn't seen him in several days. Next, she had tried the student union bars, but got the same replies. Finally, she tried the bookshops, but the story was the same there too. No one had seen him of late.

He could only be at his apartment, there was nowhere else to look, and as she had been there already and got no response, a more pronounced and deeper sense of foreboding began to develop inside her.

She went back, this time going via the caretaker's office.

Explaining to the caretaker that she was worried about her friend, who no-one had seen in several days, and who lived there, she managed to get him to agree to opening the door so she could go in and check up on him. Naturally, she had neglected to mention the parts about his dreams coming true, nor did she mention the subsequent drug use he had taken up, brought about by his fear of sleeping and the ensuing outcome of those dreams. Instead, she said he was ill and had no one to look after him, which was at least half the truth.

As soon as the apartment door had been opened, the smell assaulted them like a tidal wave. A sickening draught of putrefying flesh, marinated in urine and faecal matter hammered at their senses.

It was thick and cloying, clinging onto every molecule of air in the room and staining everything that it came into contact with, including her nasal passage.

A mere fraction of a second after the stench had hit her olfactory system, her vision was also assaulted by the image of Jonathan's body hanging from the light fitting. His face a blackened purple from the decaying blood that had pooled in his head, unable to drain due to the tourniquet created by the plastic flex tight around his throat.

For a brief moment she was paralysed with the shock of it and didn't recognise him. The question of 'what is that?' beginning to form before she realised what she was looking at. Time slowed to a crawl. It was a repulsive sight, and yet she was unable to look away, her brain caught between the disgust of it, and needing to look away, and yet, captivated by the sight.

Then, as the realisation slowly seeped through, and her mind connected the dots of what her senses were feeding it, she started to scream. It would have been a deep, guttural, primal scream that expressed the full horror of what she was experiencing.

But it was cut short.

It was cut short barely a second later as that thick putrid air was inhaled and attached itself to the back of her throat. Her taste buds instantly revolted at the attack, initiating her gag reflex to try expel the disgustingly offensive taste.

She only just managed to turn her head away to avoid adding the smell of her own vomit to the vile perfume of the air already contaminating the apartment.

The caretaker, a rough looking stocky gentleman who looked as though he had seen a thing or two in his own life, was already bent double, gagging and retching, out on the landing area, his reaction being a second or two quicker than hers.

It took them both a good few minutes to settle, and with an ashen face Elizabeth phoned the emergency services. She had no idea which one she needed, so she told the dispatch what she had before her and left it to them to send the right people. The caretaker made his excuses to leave the scene saying he needed to get some cleaning materials so he could mop up after them both.

Elizabeth curled up on the landing outside Jonathan's apartment, staring back into the room. She didn't want to, it was horrifying to her, but for an inexplicable reason, no matter how much the sight tormented and repulsed her, she still could not remove her eyes from the sight.

She didn't notice the police and paramedics arrive. She just became aware that she was no longer looking into the room, and was in the elevator going down, with a policewoman holding her shoulders. That was when she became a bit more compos mentis again. She also realised that the caretaker had not returned. He had taken himself into his own little room and begun drowning out the experiences with a bottle of rum.

Over the following weeks that led up to the funeral, Elizabeth and Jennifers friendship began to show the first signs of erosion.

There were several reasons for this, all bordering on the same issues. Jennifer was upset with Elizabeth, firstly, because it hadn't been until hours after the ambulance had taken Jonathan away that Elizabeth had bothered to call her. She felt she deserved better than that. She should have called her much sooner; Jonathan was her friend too after all. Secondly, Elizabeth had left the job of calling Jonathan's family to someone else, namely the police. She thought that was a cowardly and impersonal thing to do. One of them should have done that. If Elizabeth hadn't wanted to, then she would have. As hard as it might have been to deliver such news, they owed him that.

Elizabeth had made no reply to Jennifers admonishments, which then made Jennifer feel as though Elizabeth simply didn't care. She had just stared back at her, blankly. She may as well have been talking to a tree.

On Elizabeth's part, she thought Jennifer was being utterly unreasonable. It was easy for her to have all the answers. Hindsight is such a wonderful gift to have, especially when it's someone else's misfortune that you gain it from. But Jennifer wasn't there. She didn't see it. Didn't smell it. Didn't taste it! She didn't have the faintest idea what it was like, what such an encounter does to you. How dare she be so judgemental?

Neither of them had spoken to Jonathan's family before either, let alone met them. How was it their job to break such devastating news to them? and for it to be the first time they spoke as well! "Oh, high, I know we've never met, but your son killed himself and we only found his body several days later and it was a mess. Now you need to sort out his funeral and stuff. We thought you'd like to know, you know, seeing as he's your child that you gave birth to and loved with all your heart. Well, nice speaking to you, toodle-pip!" No, it was ridiculous to think it was their job. The police would be much better placed to do so. They could deliver the news much more gently, more diplomatically and they would have all sorts of councillors available for them, hopefully better ones than she had been offered who just sat looking at her and offered no words of comfort. Hell, she needed support herself, what good would she be trying to offer support to anyone else when she was falling apart herself? Just who did Jennifer think she was?

The seeds of resentment were well and truly sown.

Four days after the event, Elizabeth was still brooding over these thoughts and questioning how she and Jennifer ever became friends in the first place.

However, when it became apparent that they were the only two from the university going to the funeral, they had to set aside their differences, temporarily, out of respect for both Jonathan, and his family. The last thing they would need on top of burying their son would be two girls arguing with one another.

The train fare would have been prohibitively expensive for either of them to have travelled by train, so Jennifer had offered to drive the six-hour journey if they shared petrol costs. Elizabeth had agreed readily.

* * * *

The first two hours of the journey were conducted in almost complete silence, only being broken when Jennifer said she needed to pull into a service station to use the toilet.

After a short break, the next thirty minutes of the journey were also done in silence, but with the exception that the thick cloak of animosity that hung in the air was beginning to fade.

It took effort and energy to maintain such feelings, and the grief they had both been experiencing over the last couple of days, with the approach of the funeral, had drained them.

By the third hour of the journey, they had both drifted into their own thoughts, no longer making the effort to not talk to one another, when, from out of nowhere, Jennifer spoke.

"I loved him, you know."

It was neither a question, nor a statement. More a deeply suppressed thought that had taken the opportunity that the silence offered, in order to make its way to the fore, and then further seized its chances, now she had relaxed, to burst to the surface and make itself known. Jennifer took a deep breath, tightening her grip on the steering wheel as her conscious mind contemplated the confession.

She neither relaxed her grip, nor released the breath she held, for several seconds as this realisation washed over her and she came to grips with it. Then, she simultaneously relaxed her grip and her breath, as the weight of this long-suppressed feeling lifted from her as she accepted it and what it meant.

Her sense of loss multiplied, a tear formed in the crook of her eye and rolled down her cheek as though it were Sisyphus' rock, too little strength left to hold it back anymore. It was a tear slated with both joy and misery.

Elizabeth turned, thoughtfully, to face Jennifer, letting what she had just said sink in. Was this just Jennifers attempt to break the ice? It seemed a blatantly obvious statement. Of course they loved him, they had been best friends for over a year, studied together, gone almost everywhere together. On top of that, they were spending over six hours driving across country to attend his funeral. Who would do that if they didn't feel a sense of love for him?

But she wondered if there was more to it than that? Was Jennifer just trying to start a conversation in the hope that she would then ignore her in return, and thus give her a sense of superiority for not being the petty one. Some kind of pseudo-moralistic victory? Well, she wasn't about to let her get one over on her that easily.

"Me too." she replied, but with an ever so feint smugness to her tone to show she had outmanoeuvred her.

She looked harder at Jennifer to see what her next move might be. But instead of some kind of mind play, she noticed a glint of light, briefly reflected from a tear, that was rolling down her cheek as she stared blankly at the road ahead.

She wasn't playing games, that much became immediately evident. That feint smugness fell from Elizabeth's expression like a silk robe slips to the floor.

Now she wasn't sure what to say. She wanted to apologise, but if she did, it would be akin to admitting she had suspected her of trivial game playing, so instead she just waited for Jennifer to say something.

It was a long minute before she did so, and when she did, it was a distant thinking-out-loud airy kind of statement.

"No. I don't mean I loved him, I mean I *loved* him." she replied, a little more resolutely. "He was different... Nice... The kind of guy you dreamed of marrying when you were a kid, you know... Someone you trusted, someone you didn't have to worry about...someone that would be faithful to you, and only you, you know? He was that kind of guy."

"I know what you mean." Elizabeth replied, a moment later, realising that she also felt the same. "He really was one in a million."

"I wish he had have asked me out." Jennifer said, still staring out at the road ahead.

Elizabeth wasn't sure anymore if she was talking to her or talking to herself, but she couldn't contain herself.

"What are you talking about! Why would he have done that? You were constantly making fun of him, belittling him. You'd be the last person he would ask out!"

Elizabeth's outburst seemed to have very little impact on Jennifers countenance, she didn't react in any way, just kept her eyes focused on the road, still away in her own thoughts.

"I know." Jennifer replied, a heavy melancholic acceptance weighted in the words. The realisation, and regret of past actions coming home to roost, albeit way too late. "That was my stupid way of trying to show him I cared... But maybe if we had been a couple, I could have done something to help...stopped him getting onto the drugs..." her sentences drifted in and out, at the same rate her mind switched from one thought to the next as she vainly attempted to retain a coherent conversation.

Elizabeth, however, was still very much in the moment, and unable to contain her frustrations from bursting out. "How!? What could you have done? done differently to what we did? What!?" she said, angrily, raising her voice.

"I don't know..." Jennifer replied, so faintly she was almost exhaling the words. "I really don't know...I just wish..."

Defeat and exasperation stained every word she uttered, and she let them trail off as she disappeared back into her own tormented mind.

Deep down, Elizabeth knew just what Jennifer meant. She wished too. Wished they could have done something differently. Wished she could alleviate the feelings of guilt that were such a burden on her shoulders. She wished she had someone to blame. Not just blame them, but extract some kind of revenge on them.

But she couldn't.

Nor could she realise, in her grief, that this complex web of emotions was causing her to lay the blame squarely at the feet of the one person who actually knew how she felt, who might be able to offer some help, or even just give a little mutual consolation. Even if neither of them could ever express the full extent of it, they would at least know how the other felt. But they couldn't, so they took the easy way out and blamed one another.

Not too long after the funeral, Elizabeth moved out of the flat that she and Jennifer had shared for the last year or more.

For the first time in a while, there was no argument between the two of them when she broke the news. They both accepted that it was the right thing to do. They hadn't exchanged anything more than the most minimal of polite pleasantries with one another for some time; so, they simply moved on with their lives and went their separate ways.

Reading Group Questions

1 - What moral dilemmas do you see within the book? and how would you decide what to do in those situations?

2 - What do you think the following characters represent
(a) Josh
(b) The Auburn-Haired Girl
(c) the mysterious man in the bookshop/2nd hand shop

3 - What is your interpretation of the dream in Chapter 8?

4 - What is your interpretation of the dream in Chapter 16?

5 - How is the book symbolic of life in general?

Select Bibliography

The following books were read for additional information and my personal understanding in the writing of this novel. For those of a more studious nature, you can read any of these (some are more readily available than others) if you wish to gain a greater understanding of aspects of this work.

- Memories, Dreams and reflections: C.G. Jung
- Social Psychology (2nd Ed): Tony Malim
- The Interpretation of Dreams: S. Freud
- Sleep and Dreams: A. Maury
- The Human Brain: New Scientist-The collection Vol2

www.ingramcontent.com/pod-product-compliance
Lightning Source LLC
Chambersburg PA
CBHW010406310726
48979CB00012B/2142/J

* 9 7 8 1 9 1 7 4 2 5 3 7 7 *